ALL FOR THIS

Here and Now series, book three

ALL FOR THIS

Here and Now series, book three

New York Times Bestselling Author
LEXI RYAN

Interior designed and formatted by E.M. Tippetts Book Designs

For Annie. You're a great cheerleader, and when it comes to brainstorming, you're the bee's knees. But mostly, I'm just glad that, after all this time, I can still call you my friend. Love and miss you.

ONE

NATE

She's wearing his ring.

Hanna's hand shakes as she presses it to her lips and her engagement ring flashes at me. She's in a thin pink robe, her hair falling in wild waves around her shoulders. Max stiffens next to her, bare-chested and protective. It doesn't take a genius to know what they were doing before they answered the door.

The sucker punch to the gut is too much, and I take a step back despite myself.

I shouldn't have come here. LA is too insane right now and I need to lie low until this madness settles. But I never should have come to Hanna's apartment.

It was instinct. As soon as I talked to Vivian and made arrangements for Collin, I came here.

"You're supposed to be dead," Hanna whispers.

"I'm not." But I can't decide if she wishes I were.

Our eyes are locked. I need to break free and leave—go back to Asher's and hide from the world while I wait for Collin to arrive.

Max turns to the living room, where he clicks on the TV, and while I'm trapped in the torment in her eyes, the news anchor tells the world that I'm alive and well.

Hanna finally releases me from her gaze and whips around to take in the TV, as if it might provide her with better evidence than my standing in her doorway.

"I just wanted to make sure you're okay." The lie scrapes across my heart as it passes my lips. I wanted so much more than to make sure she was okay. There's something about discovering that you should be dead that changes the way you look at the world. Changes what you're willing to risk.

"I'm okay," she says, her gaze still on the TV screen.

Suddenly, she throws her hand over her mouth and runs to the bathroom, and the sounds of her retching carry down the hallway.

Max throws me a look I don't understand. Maybe he too needs confirmation that I'm really at their door. Then he follows her.

When they return, his arm is wrapped around her shoulders, and she's leaning against his chest. I want to rip him off her and take her into my arms, where she belongs, but she sinks into his embrace as if she needs him to stand. Another reminder that I don't belong here.

Hanna might be the best thing that ever happened to me, but maybe for her, that's Max. Hell, Asher told me Max was no money-grubbing asshole after Hanna for the wrong reasons. And I already suspected that, didn't I? It was just further evidence.

And here he is—fucking Good Guy of the Year—holding her up when her lover stands at the door.

My hardened heart threatens to crumble.

Fuck. "I'll be at Asher's if you need me." I nod and back away as Max stares at me, his face a mask, his eyes unreadable.

I rush down the stairs before my heart can keep me where my brain knows I don't belong.

HANNA

He's gone. He came long enough to turn my world upside down and then disappeared.

Max kisses the top of my head, and I'm so conflicted by the

intimacy of that single gesture. I want to curl into his sweetness, let him protect me the way I know he wants to. And at the same time, I want to push him away and tell him that he can't touch me like that anymore. Because Nate is alive.

"What can I do?" Max asks.

I shake my head and make my way to the bedroom to get dressed. "I need to go after him." I pull on a pair of jeans and a T-shirt and slide into my tennis shoes. When I reach the front door, I sense Max behind me and stop. "Will you be here when I get back?"

He's silent for a beat, and for the space of a breath, I wish we could go back to the simplicity of the moments before Nate knocked on my door. The wish disintegrates the moment I think it. Even the part of me that loves Max and craves a life with him wants Nate alive.

"Do you want me to be?" Max asks.

"Is it that simple?"

"For me it is. If you want me to be here, I will be."

I meet his eyes for the first time since our world imploded. "It's not that simple for me."

"I love you," he whispers. He hands me my car keys then reaches around me and opens the door. "Be careful."

I pocket my keys to appease him, but I have no intention of taking my car. I walk through the darkness, taking the path along the river and hoping the cadence of my steps might calm the riot in my heart.

I find Nate standing on the dock near Asher's house, his hands wrapped around the railing as he looks across the water. I knew he'd be here. Did he know I'd come after him?

The wind runs its fingers through his tousled hair, and I'm so overwhelmed with the need to touch him—to make sure he's real and alive and healthy. I shove my hands into my pockets so they can't betray me.

"You lied to me."

He nods without turning to me. "Seemed like the right thing to do at the time." His deep murmur floats on the breeze and wraps me in its embrace. Right now, Nate's voice is the most beautiful sound in the world, the only thing I want to hear.

"I understand why you would lie to me about taking my virginity if you thought I was going to marry Max," I say, standing next to him at the rail. "I don't agree with the decision, but I understand. But you lied to me about what was between us—about what you'd been willing to have with me. Why?"

"You'd made your choice," he whispers, his knuckles tightening around the wood.

I shake my head. "Not when I came to LA. I'd called it off with Max, and you made me believe that you'd never changed your mind about us."

"Did you really call it off, Hanna? Did you tell people you weren't going to marry him? Or was it a secret again?"

"I…" I force my lungs to take air. "That's not fair. You knew I couldn't remember, and you lied."

He studies me for a minute. "And how much do you remember?"

"I remember the day we made love. I remember you telling me that it was time for me to make a choice."

"After that?"

I shake my head. "Nothing."

He looks back to the water. "Let's just say that by the time you left my place, it was pretty clear I couldn't give you what you wanted. And after five days of you not answering my calls or texts…"

"Yet a week later, you were at my house, climbing into my bed?"

"Foolish optimism."

"What happened? Why did you have to lie?"

"I was right, wasn't I? It didn't take you long to take him back." His gaze flicks to my hand, and I realize his jaw is hard—angry. "You didn't wait long to put his ring back on your finger. I'm not the only one who lied."

The wind whips my hair around my face and stings my eyes. "What's that supposed to mean?"

"You're fucking kidding me, right? You took off his ring and told me you weren't going to marry him. But what you really meant was that you wanted your rebound boy again. That's all I am to you, the guy you like to screw around with when Max hurts your feelings."

"That's unfair," I breathe.

"Is it? How long after my supposed death did you wait to fuck him, Hanna?"

Hanna. Not *angel.* I've lost that label. "You walked away from me."

"I didn't walk away. I let you go."

"What's the difference?"

He shakes his head. "Go home. I'm sorry I interrupted you. Go back to fucking your fiancé."

His words hurt. They make me feel dirty and ashamed when I've done nothing wrong.

"Why did you even come here tonight? To hurt me? To make me feel guilty? Mission. Accomplished."

He turns and closes the distance between us, sliding his fingers into my hair and cupping my jaw in his hands. "I came because I thought you would be grieving me and I couldn't stand the idea of you hurting." His eyes dip to my mouth. "But I guess I didn't need to worry about that."

I swallow hard and wait for my feet to obey my mind—to back away before he can kiss me. But they don't. I've never had any willpower to resist this man, and I wonder if that weakness will be my undoing.

"You have no idea what the last ten days have been like for me."

"No. I guess Max is the only one who knows that." When he lifts his eyes back to mine, the pain there rips me in two.

"I won't apologize for loving him. He's a good man."

"I'm glad," he says. "I hope you two have a good life."

Another punch in the gut, but my gut's practically numb by now, so I hardly wince. "So this is it, then? You're just going to show up on my doorstep—alive when you're supposed to be dead—make me feel like shit, and then walk away?"

He leans his forehead against mine and our breath mingles. His hands tighten in my hair almost painfully. "Are you asking me to do something else?"

"No," I whisper, and that's it. That's all I have left. All my will and all my strength go into that single word.

He releases me and steps back. I wait for relief, but it doesn't come. His eyes are resting on my left hand, and I want to cut it off for the pain it puts on his face.

"Goodbye, Hanna."

TWO

MAX

The clock's second hand mocks me as I sit in Hanna's otherwise silent apartment and wait for her to return.

I wanted to tell her not to go, but I knew she needed to. I wanted to go with her, but I would have just been in the way.

What the hell am I going to do now?

I'm not a fool. I know she still loves him, and I know she wouldn't still be wearing my ring if he hadn't been presumed dead. What I don't know is how this changes things. Am I supposed to step aside so she can be with the father of her children? Am I supposed to hold on tight and pretend it doesn't kill me to see the way she looks at him—as if he's some gift, a miracle from the heavens? As if no one and nothing exists for her when he's near?

In the cupboard, I find the wrapped jewelry box I positioned by the coffee and tuck it into my pocket. I have epically bad timing. I'd just gotten the ring and made plans to propose when Meredith decided to throw a wrench in my world, and tonight, I'd hidden the house key when Nate showed up at her door.

I shouldn't have signed the lease, but it seemed like the perfect surprise. We spend more nights together than apart, and I hate the idea of her using those stairs several times a day. And with the babies coming…

The door groans softly as it opens. Hanna's face is pale, her cheeks wet with tears.

I stand without thinking.

What a fucking asshole. It's all I can do not to track him down and punch him in the face. Because she's standing here pale and limp, and he did that to her. He showed up on her doorstep without warning and then walked away like he didn't just turn her world upside down. And whatever he said when she went to find him made her cry. *Asshole.*

I wrap my arms around her and she clings to me—her nose against my chest, her hands curling around my arms. I stroke her hair and wait for her to break down, for these quiet tears to turn to sobs. But they don't. She just holds on, her slow and steady breaths warming my chest.

"How did my life get so screwed up?"

"Are you okay?"

When she lifts her eyes to mine, there's so much sadness in them that it makes my chest ache. "Can you forgive me for loving him too?" she asks. "Can we really survive this?"

Relief hits me center mass and splinters out through my limbs. Because there's still a *we.* I bring her hand to my mouth and press my lips to her knuckles. If I could package the intensity of my love in a single gesture, if I could prove to her how hard I'm willing to hold on, she wouldn't doubt us for a second.

When she settles her head against my chest again, I squeeze my eyes shut and say a prayer that I'll be enough for her.

"I'm not going anywhere," I whisper into her hair.

NATE

"Fuck, it's good to see you." Asher pulls me in for a hug and slaps me on the back.

"You too."

Maggie waits behind him, half sniffling, half smiling, and

when Asher doesn't release me soon enough for her liking, she pulls him off me and curls into me. "You scared the shit out of us," she growls into my chest.

I grin and stroke her hair. "I think your girl likes me, Asher."

He grunts, and Maggie says, "Shut up, Crane. You couldn't handle me."

"No doubt," I mutter.

She pulls out of my arms, grabs me by the wrist, and leads me into the kitchen while Asher takes my bags up the stairs.

After pouring herself a shot of tequila, she hands one to me. I throw it back without question. I haven't had anything alcoholic to drink since the night Hanna showed up at my house in LA, only half of her memory intact. I relish the warmth of the alcohol as it sinks to my stomach.

"What the fuck happened?" she asks. "How was it that you weren't on that helicopter?"

Asher joins us and stands so Maggie's back is against his chest. They're so damn good for each other, it eats at me.

"I was supposed to be," I begin. I pour myself another shot because, fuck, if anything calls for alcohol abuse, it's finding out that you're supposed to be dead and the woman you love—the woman who's the only reason you aren't dead right along with the rest of your tour—has moved on with another man. "I decided I couldn't do the tour and chartered a private plane to get me to Janelle in India. She was at this spiritual retreat and I was staying there, but they don't allow technology, so I…I had no idea the helicopter went down until someone arrived to deliver the news of my death to Janelle."

"Where is Janelle?" Maggie asks.

"She's still there. I told her to stay, and she was shaken enough that she didn't feel like she wanted to be anywhere else."

"Why couldn't you do the tour?" Asher asks.

Maggie says, "Because of Hanna, I bet."

I look to Asher, who shakes his head. He didn't tell her.

"Why would you say that?" I ask Maggie.

"I know about you and Hanna. Everyone knows." She digs through a stack of magazines and hands me one.

My gut burns when I see it. "Fucking privacy-invading assholes," I growl. My gaze snaps back to Maggie. "Max knows too?"

"Yeah," Maggie says.

Then she smacks me on the right shoulder. "That's for scaring me." Then again on the left. "And that's for screwing around with my sister and not even telling me about it."

Asher grabs Maggie's wrists and pulls her back against his chest. "Quit beating on the company." Then to me, he says, "You can stay as long as you want. When will Collin get here?"

"Vivian's bringing him in the morning."

Maggie's eyes fill. "That poor kid. I can't imagine what a rollercoaster this has been for him."

My throat is too thick, and I can't risk speaking, so I only nod. Vivian said Collin never cried. He insisted Daddy wasn't dead because Daddy would never leave him without saying goodbye.

One impulsive decision is the only reason my son still has his father, and that fact makes me feel so insanely helpless I want to scream.

"I'm ready for him to be here," I finally say. "And thanks for letting us stay awhile. LA is a madhouse. Vivian's been hounded by paparazzi since the helicopter went down."

Asher nods. "Of course. You're welcome as long as you want."

We all say our goodnights, and the happy couple makes their way to their bedroom, leaving me with the bottle of tequila and memories of Hanna's mouth under mine.

NATE

Five Days Before Hanna's Accident

"Stay one more night?"

She rolls to face me and runs her fingers over my stubble. I need a shave, but I can't bring myself to have a smooth face when Hanna's around. She can't keep her hands off my face when it's a little rough.

"You're sure you want to be with me before I've made my choice?"

My gut burns. Of course, I want her to make her choice *now*. I want to be the easy choice and for her to say she doesn't need to think about it. But it's not that simple. Hanna's heart is too loyal for that, and that's what I love about her, isn't it? Her big heart. Her loyalty. And a goodness that runs so deep and so steady that, when she's close, it becomes part of who *I* am.

"Stay with me. One more night," I repeat, and the unsaid words *in case this is goodbye* electrify the air between us.

I trace my hand down her body, and the tension seeps out of her with a soft moan that gets me hard every time. Maybe I shouldn't have taken her virginity. Maybe she'll regret that after she leaves, but I know I never will. Being inside her, watching the pleasure wash over her face as her body adjusted to mine and I finally sank deep... It was the most beautiful gift I've ever been given, second only to a woman like her loving me.

She grabs the tequila we left on the bedside table last night and says, "Cheers," before taking a swig.

Taking the bottle, I grin and splash some between her breasts. "Cheers," I murmur before I lick away the liquid, following it as it trails down her belly and sides. By the time I'm done, she's squirming under me.

Gently, I cup her between her legs, where she's wet from our lovemaking. "Are you sore?"

She shrugs. "A little, but it's not a bad feeling. More like muscles after a long workout. The good kind of hurt."

The good kind of hurt. Yeah, I'm feeling that too, even if my pain is more of the existential variety.

"Hmm." I roll on top of her and pin her hands to the bed as I murmur against her skin and kiss my way down her body. "Let me kiss it and make it better." Releasing her hands only so I can part her thighs, I sink to my stomach on the bed and position my head between her legs. "Right here?" I trace her opening, and she gasps and parts her legs farther.

When I replace my fingers with my mouth, she fists her hands in my hair, and *fuck,* do I love that. I stroke her with my fingers and tongue until she's moaning and so close to coming that she's fucking my face with jerking, desperate movements. Only then do I pull away and slide back up the bed next to her body.

"Better?"

She pries her eyes open and frowns at me. "You're...you're done?"

I have to laugh. "You're so fucking cute when you're trying to pretend you don't care about getting off."

"I don't want to be...greedy. I mean, I know we just had sex, so maybe you're not interested."

I grunt and lead her hand to my aching erection. "I'm interested, angel. With you, I'm always *interested.*"

She licks her lips as she wraps her fingers around me and strokes. "Then why did you stop again?"

My hips thrust, moving in her hand. "Because I want to be inside you when you come but I don't want to make you too sore. I'm trying to be a gentleman."

"A gentleman? Oh." She releases me, and I nearly grunt in disappointment. "In that case, I'm going to be a lady. And this lady needs a shower."

I stay in bed as she saunters into the bathroom. Not because I'm going to lose the opportunity to shower with Hanna—fuck no—but because I like watching her ass jiggle as she walks. There are very few perfect sights in this world of imperfections, and as such, I will never take Hanna's ass for granted.

By the time I pull myself out of bed and meet her in the bathroom, she's already in the shower, water sluicing over her curves. I'm jealous of the damn water because it's touching her everywhere I want to. I'm going to have to lap it all up with my tongue.

I step in behind her and press my mouth to her neck, sucking at the sensitive spot before knotting my hand in her wet hair and turning her to face me. "I love you," I say against her mouth.

"I love you too."

The tenderness that swamps me is terrifying. I don't want to let her go, and the fear that I might have to consumes me. I slant my mouth over hers, pouring everything I have into the kiss—all my love and fear, my vulnerability and desperation. I can't handle the power of what I'm feeling, so I put it into my kiss.

Soon, her back is against the glass, her leg is hitched around my waist, and my dick is nestled right against her hot, slick pussy.

"Mine," I growl against her lips.

Then I slide into her and it feels so fucking good I almost come right then and there. I lift her other leg—greedy for more, desperate to bury myself as deep in her as possible—and I fuck her against the glass. Her mouth is on my neck, her hands in my hair, her ankles locked behind my back.

"Mine," I repeat.

Her moan echoes in the shower, but I need more. I wrap my hand under her thigh and stroke her where our bodies are joined. Her pussy squeezes around me violently, and she bites the side of my neck as she rides out her orgasm. And I'm so wild with lust and jealousy and this soul-shredding love I feel for her that I've come inside her before I realize I'm not wearing a condom.

I pull out of her and slowly help her feet to the ground. "I'm sorry," I whisper.

She cocks her head. "Why? That was…amazing." She winces a little. "Okay, so I'm sore, but it's really okay."

I drag a hand through my hair. The shower is still running, and I turn it off before I answer. "I'm sorry because I wasn't wearing a condom."

Her lips part as she registers my words.

"There's probably nothing to worry about," I say, but I'm thinking of the one other time in my life when I forgot to wear a condom. I was nineteen, and nine months later, Collin was born. Best mistake I've ever made, but still. "We'll be more careful. Are you… You're on something, right?"

She opens her mouth and closes it. Goose bumps prickle on her arms as she shivers. I lead her out of the shower and wrap her in a towel.

"I'm sorry," she says. "I didn't even think…"

Oh, damn. "*You're* sorry? Angel, you didn't do anything wrong. I should have…" Then it hits me. "You're *not* on birth control."

She shakes her head, and I pull her against my chest and squeeze my eyes shut, cursing myself over and over in my mind. I want Hanna. I want to find a way to make it work with her. But another kid? That's leaps and bounds beyond what I'm ready for. *Fuck it.* I can't even let my thoughts go there.

"It's going to be okay," I promise. "The chances of this resulting in an accidental pregnancy are so small."

She wraps her arms around her middle, holding the towel against her breasts. She studies the floor. "What would happen if I were? What if we had shitty luck and the small chance turns into a baby?" When she looks up at me through water-dampened lashes, I can see the confusion in her eyes.

"It'll be okay."

"But what if it's not?"

Fuck, fuck, fuck. "Do we really have to have this conversation right now? Isn't that just borrowing trouble?"

She squeezes her eyes shut and turns away from me. "I'm not trying to be melodramatic, but it matters."

"I won't ruin today. I'm not going to have a fight over nothing."

"Why does it have to be a fight? I'm just asking what you'd do. What *we'd* do."

"We'd figure it out. I have more than enough room here. You could move in with me or—"

"You think I'd move to LA?" The horror in her voice is a backhand to the face, a reminder of all the reasons I've kept this part of my life inaccessible to women. She points to the bedroom. "Is that what you meant when you said I had to choose? You want me to give up my life for you?"

"I didn't say that."

"But you're saying it now, aren't you?"

I set my jaw. I wish she'd turn around and look at me. "I said I want to find a way to make it work. I don't know what that looks like because I've never allowed myself to consider it."

"Consider it now," she whispers. "In your mind, do I have to give up my bakery and move to LA if we're going to be together?"

"My son is here," I say slowly. "So in my mind, that's the easiest solution. Can we please end this conversation? We're arguing over a hypothetical—"

"No. This isn't just a hypothetical. This is something I need to know." She squeezes herself tightly and lowers her head. "If I'm going to choose, I need to know."

I spin her around and squeeze her shoulders as I growl, "*I. Love. You.*" Anger tears through me with my frustration. I want my love to be enough for her. *I* want to be enough for her. But here we are, minutes after making love, and she's holding me up to this other guy. "Why can't that be enough for you? Not forever but for now. *Please.*"

She lifts her eyes to mine, and pain slices through my gut at the doubt I see there. Doubt in *us*. Doubt in *me*. "I think it's time for me to look beyond here and now. Here and now is all I let myself think about this summer, and look where that got me."

I flinch. "It got you here. With me. Is that so terrible?"

"And what happens next year? The year after that? What happens when I'm ready to have the house with the picket fence and you're still in LA? What happens when I'm ready for babies?"

"Don't do this. Don't destroy what's between us by asking it to carry more than it can hold. This is new, and it's not fair to push it like this."

"You're the one who told me you wanted me to choose," she whispers. "These are things I need to think about."

I crush my mouth to hers and yank the towel from her body. I expect her to push me away, but I'm wrong. Jesus, am I wrong. She's just as greedy for me as I am for her. Her hands go to my hair. Her breasts press against my chest. Her tongue slides against mine, desperate. This is where we've always been good. There's never been a question of the heat between us. Here's where we can always find our way—this kiss, the heat of our bare skin pressed together. How can this be so powerful and mean nothing? I know it's the question we're both asking ourselves as terror holds us in its steely grip.

"Was it like this with him?" I ask against her ear, my hand skimming her side. "Did you need him the way you need me?"

"Don't."

"You didn't, Hanna. There's a reason *I'm* the one you let kiss you here." I settle my hand between her legs, and her eyes float closed. "There's a reason you never fucked him and were ready to let me inside you the first night we met."

"It's different."

"Damn straight it is." I want to slide my fingers inside her, feel the slick walls of her heat, feel evidence of the need I won't let her dismiss. But I know she's gotta be sore and I settle for cupping her and the satisfaction of the needy rocking of her hips. "It's different because you're *mine* more than you were ever his. You might love him, but you *need* me. And if you choose him, you'll always wonder if you and I could have made it work."

She wraps her hand around my wrist and slowly removes it from between her legs before stepping back. "And what if I choose you? Will I spend the rest of my life wondering if I could have a family and kids if I'd chosen him?"

I fist my hands at my sides because I'm afraid that, if I let myself touch her, I'll pull her into my arms and refuse to let her go. I'm afraid one hit of her scent will make me promise things I know I can't give.

"I don't want any more kids, Hanna. I have Collin and I can't do that to him."

"Can't or won't?"

"Don't," I plead.

"There's a difference," she whispers. "An important one."

"Maybe I'll change my mind, but right now..."

She swallows and her eyes well with tears. "Thank you for your honesty." Then she leaves the bathroom.

I feel like an idiot and an asshole, but I won't lie to win her. She deserves better.

After I wash my face and dry off, I return to the bedroom. She's dressed and her bag is thrown over her shoulder.

"Hanna, I'm sorry."

She shakes her head. "Don't apologize for being honest."

"If I changed my mind for anyone, it would be for you. Don't go. Not yet."

"I'm going to fly home tonight. I need to think."

Stepping forward, I cup her jaw in my hands and tilt her face up to mine. "I wish I'd met you before you started dating him."

"And I wish we could just be a normal couple in love. But we're not." She touches her hand to my cheek. "There's never been anything normal about us."

"Only because this is better than normal. You know it is."

"Give me time. I need to think."

She's ending this. She's fucking leaving me and ending this. "Don't do this. Hanna..."

"We'll talk when you get back from London." She turns toward the door.

"Angel," I call. She stops but doesn't turn to me. "You can leave, but you're taking my heart with you. You can choose him, but part of you will always be mine."

THREE

HANNA

The first time Max and I made love, I told him I'd never had sex without a condom.

I was wrong.

I lie in bed with the memory searing my brain like a hot iron. When I close my eyes, I can feel the goose bumps on my arms, the cool tile under my feet, my skin still wet, my body sore from making love to Nate, my legs sore from being wrapped around his waist as he took me in the shower.

"I don't want any more kids, Hanna. I have Collin and I can't do that to him."

Then when I returned to LA after the amnesia, when we were saying goodbye, he met me in the shower again. *"Why'd you have to forget?"* At the time I thought he meant *forget us*, but he meant more than that. He meant…everything. His offering more, his taking my virginity, his making love to me in the shower and the conversation that rendered him silent when he discovered I'd made my choice.

I settle my hand on my stomach and imagine the little lives growing inside. My pregnancy was hard for me to accept, and the idea of having a baby at all—let alone twins—still terrifies me. But, despite all of that, these babies feel like a miracle and a gift to me. And to Nate, they'll be nothing more than a slight to his firstborn.

When my alarm goes off, I'm relieved. I may have spent more of the night pretending to sleep than actually sleeping.

Max reaches for me as I slide out of bed, and I squeeze his hand before padding through the dark to get ready in the bathroom. If I worried that he'd want to have sex last night, I needn't have. He held me in his arms and fell asleep, and I lay there wondering how I ever made a choice between two halves of my heart.

In the bakery, I find comfort in my morning routine—warming the ovens, pulling the ingredients for today's recipes, listing the outside orders for the following week, and penning them into my schedule.

As I bake, my mind turns, and to keep myself from spinning my emotional wheels, I make a mental list of what I know to be true.

I chose Max once and I have no reason to doubt that decision given what I know now about the bakery and how he feels about me. Especially considering Nate doesn't want any more children and I always hoped to have a big family.

Max is exactly what I need now. My future with him will be stable and secure, and most importantly, it's a future here, at home.

Despite all of that, I find myself trying to make the choice all over again. Maybe because I'm pregnant with Nate's babies and that complicates things. Or maybe for another reason altogether.

I need to tell Nate about the pregnancy, regardless of how he feels about having more children. When I talked to him last night, I was still trying to digest the fact that he was alive. And trying to defend myself against his accusations. He thinks I just jumped into bed with Max the second I learned his helicopter went down. It's not that simple—nothing is. He walked away from me. He said goodbye.

I would have ended up with Max again, even if the whole world hadn't thought Nate was dead.

Wouldn't I?

And it's in the space of that tiny question, in the hesitation between the beats of my heart, that my kernel of guilt sprouts poisonous blossoms in my heart and leaves my relationship with Max in its shadow.

Telling Nate about the babies while keeping Max's ring on my finger is about the cruelest position I could put him in. I'll be making him the second family—again and forever—when he deserves so much more.

At six, I go to the front to unlock the door and turn on the sign, and I find my mother standing at the entrance in her church clothes. The moment I open the door for her, she wraps me in her arms.

I will never be too old or too broken to be soothed by the comfort of my mother's arms. She strokes my hair, and I let quiet tears leak from my eyes.

"I might not approve of your relationship with that rock star," she whispers, "but I thank God my grandbabies won't be deprived of knowing their father."

That makes me cry harder.

She smooths my hair and gently pats my back. "How's Max holding up?"

I withdraw from her embrace. "He's fine." And he is. Poor guy doesn't even get the opportunity to be pissed off. If Nate had never been presumed dead, no one would have questioned Max's right to be angry as hell about my summer with Nate. Maybe it wasn't cheating, but it wasn't honest either. And that was stolen from him. Since Max isn't enough of an asshole to wish someone dead, he's left having to be okay with Nate's reappearance in our lives.

"I just don't understand," Mom says as she walks over to the coffeepot.

I get to work on filling the bakery cases. "Don't understand what?"

"How all of this happened. The pregnancy, the postponed wedding, your whole relationship with Nate Crane. A few days before your accident, you couldn't *wait* to marry Max."

I freeze with a tray of scones in my hands. "I couldn't?"

"The sooner the better, you told me. You weren't even wearing a ring yet, but you just wanted to start your life with him."

"I said that?" I whisper.

"Yes. And it didn't surprise me that you felt that way. Of course you would. You and Max were always so good together." She looks down at her coffee and draws in a breath. "Then you had that horrible accident. You seemed so reluctant to make wedding plans, but I thought it was because you couldn't remember. Then, suddenly, you were pregnant with another man's baby. It didn't make sense to me."

"When did I tell you I wanted to marry Max?" I ask, pressing. Would I have told her that to help with his chances to get the grant? No. That doesn't make sense. She would have been just as likely to support Max as my boyfriend as she would have if he were my fiancé.

Mom frowns at me. "Shortly before your accident."

"But *when*?" I squeak. Mentally, I'm calculating what I know, what I remember, and trying to fit it in.

Mom props her hands on her hips. "Why does it matter?"

"I still don't remember everything," I explain. "And those last four days are still completely gone. I want to know."

Her eyes tilt to the ceiling. "Well, I guess it was after Abby's party. The day after, maybe? Because you'd forgotten to bring her gift to the party and you were swinging by the house to drop one off. Gosh, you know, maybe it was the day before your accident. That evening."

"And I wasn't wearing the ring?"

She shakes her head. "The first time I saw your ring, you were in the hospital. Why don't you ask Max when he proposed? He can fill in some details."

Because he proposed months before.

Mom cocks her head. "You look pale, Hanna. Are you sleeping enough? You need to make sleep a priority for those babies. Pregnancy is hard on the body."

"I will," I promise. I hand her a cup of coffee and lead her out the door.

It's so tempting to hold on to the secret as long as I can. I force myself to pick up my phone and text Nate.

NATE

"Daddy!"

My heart swells as Collin runs to me across Asher's backyard. I squat and open my arms, and he throws himself in them, hugging me as I lift him off the ground. I can breathe easier when he's close to me. He's the reminder of all the reasons I needed to let Hanna go. All the reasons I should wish her well in her life with Max. He's the only thing that matters.

"I knew you weren't dead," Collin says, his face buried in my neck. "I just knew it."

I stroke his dark hair, close my eyes, and say a prayer. "I love you, buddy."

He gives me one more squeeze before pulling back and grinning at me. "Mommy said I can stay here for a while. Is that true? Do I get to sleep over at Uncle Asher's house?"

Five minutes ago, I didn't feel like smiling, but Collin's happiness is contagious, and nothing matters now that he's here—safe and with me, where he belongs.

"It's true," I answer. "How was the flight?"

"Awesome! Mommy let me drink champagne and then she played DS with me! Did you know she can beat all the levels on *Luigi's Mansion*?"

I lift my gaze to Vivian, who followed Collin into the yard. "Ginger ale," she explains. "Extra yummy in a champagne flute."

"Drake," I say, nodding to her personal security guard.

The tall man straightens his sleek leather jacket and nods as a greeting. He's been Vivian's bodyguard since we were teenagers, and I've seen him bloody faces of men who dared get their hands or their cameras too close to Vivian. His flowing, platinum-blond hair and ghostly blue eyes make him a more likely candidate for a retro romance novel cover than a security guard, but he's good at his job.

"Is that Collin I see out there?" Asher calls from the patio.

"It is!" Collin squirms, and I set him on his feet so he can run after "Uncle" Asher.

"Thanks for bringing him," I tell Vivian. After over a week in silence, speaking still feels odd. When I went to India to join Janelle at her little spiritual retreat, I had no idea I'd be handing over my electronics and my right to speak for the foreseeable future. Not that I cared. I didn't want to talk to anyone anyway.

"The last thing you needed was a paparazzo catching your reunion or, worse, following you here. It was better this way."

I nod, watching as Collin follows Asher into the house. "Jamaal will be here soon, and Asher and I are hiring extra security. They'll find me here, but I don't have to let them get close."

Her shoulders drop a little, and I know she's relieved. She's never been fond of what she sees as my "lax" security measures. "I'm glad to hear it."

"How's he handling the divorce?" I ask, looking at Collin.

She shrugs and puts on the brave smile I recognize so well. "Better than expected, I guess. Except he seems to think this means you and I are getting back together, and I try to explain that sometimes mommies and daddies love each other but can't be together."

"Viv," I whisper.

She shakes her head. "Don't apologize. That makes me feel worse."

"I need to apologize, especially about what happened in London. It was—"

She puts her fingers to my lips. "Stop while you're ahead. Please. I'm just glad you're not dead. The rest is irrelevant."

I pull her into a hug and press a kiss to the top of her head. "I'll always love you. You gave me my son."

"Be careful."

"I'm not getting in a helicopter anytime soon, so you don't need to—"

"With *her*, Nathaniel. Be careful with that girl. I don't trust her."

"Hanna?"

She nods. "I don't want to see you hurt."

Too late. "You're the one who insisted I tell her how I feel."

"That was before I knew she was seeing someone else. I saw

them together."

"I know about her fiancé, Viv. Just…back off, okay?"

"She's engaged to him?" She smacks me in the chest. "Why are you messing around with a woman who's engaged to someone else?"

"She wasn't engaged then."

My phone buzzes. Hanna's name scrolls across the screen, making my gut flip and clench all in one riotous movement. All summer long, texts from Hanna were the highlight of my days. How long has it been since I received a text message from her?

Hanna: *Can we talk tonight?*
Nate: *What's there to say?*
Hanna: *Please.*

I swallow as I stare at the single word in her last message. *Please.* I can't say no to her, even if seeing her with his ring on her finger will kill something inside me.

"Is that her?" Vivian asks. She reaches for my phone, and I sidestep her.

"Back off, Viv. Don't try to mother-bear me. This doesn't concern you."

"You said you told her how you felt."

"I did," I growl. "Drop it."

"You see? It's better. Now you know and—"

I don't hear the rest because I'm walking away. The last thing I need right now is to hear Vivian's opinion of my relationship with Hanna. When I'm alone in the house again, I reply to Hanna's last text.

Nate: *The dock. Nine thirty.*

FOUR

MAX

"How are you holding up?"

I'm quiet for a minute, looking around Brady's. There have been plenty of curious glances thrown my way since William and I sat down with our beer. The news of Hanna's and my canceled wedding spread across town like the best kind of gossip.

By now, half the town knows Hanna is pregnant with another man's baby, though I'm not sure who leaked that information. Not that it was a secret, but the summer breakup was. The story of her pregnancy is irresistible to the gossip hounds.

"I'm good," I finally say. William is studying me as if he doesn't trust my words. "Relieved, honestly."

He raises a brow. "Yeah?"

I'm not sure how to explain it. I want Hanna, but I want her to be with me because I'm her choice, not because a tragedy made me the default choice. Every night I slept with her in my arms felt like a miracle made possible by the death of someone she loved. His death tainted what we had.

I only say, "It's better this way."

"You two are okay?"

I wish I knew. "She's still in love with him."

"She's still in love with you, too," Will says, and I nod because that's what I've been holding on to. "Where is she tonight?"

"She's meeting Nate." I swallow. "She needs to tell him about the babies." I offered to go with her. I wanted him to see that I'm standing by her side through all of this, but she declined. *"Having you there will just hurt him more."*

"He's going to fight for her," Will warns.

"I'll fight harder."

Will grins his approval.

I have to change the subject. If I think too much about Hanna meeting Nate tonight, I'll lose my mind. "How's Cally feeling?"

Will beams at the mention of his pregnant wife. "Tired, nauseated, anxious to grow a belly so the whole world knows she's pregnant. How's Hanna?"

"Same. Tired. The nausea comes and goes, but cold washcloths help a lot."

"Shit," Will grumbles, looking to the door. "We have company."

"Hi, boys." Meredith is all smiles as she slides into the booth next to me. She smells of rum and her eyes are drunken and glazed. "I heard the good news about Nate Crane. Didn't you?"

William stiffens. He and Meredith used to be friends—more, even—but after the way she treated Cally, he can't stand her anymore. "I don't remember inviting you to join us."

"Where's Claire?" I ask. I refuse to take her bait, and she scowls.

"I dropped her off at your mom's."

My jaw ticks in annoyance. "I thought you were going to spend some time with her before your business trip."

"Don't tell me how to be a mother and I won't tell you how to be a fiancé. You are still engaged, aren't you? Or has she come to her senses and left town with that sexy rock star?"

"Go away, Meredith," Will mutters.

She ignores him and looks at me. "Is it true you rented the old Blackman house?"

"It is."

"Well…I'm pretty sure once Nate Crane finds out your *fiancée* is pregnant with his babies, you're not going to have the need for three bedrooms anymore."

"Go. Away," Will repeats, and I add, "What he said."

She shrugs and slides out of the booth.

Will watches her go, only turning back to me when he's convinced she's far enough away. "She's poison. I know she's the mother of your child, but you need to find a way to keep her from contaminating your relationship with Hanna."

Across the bar, Meredith is flirting with a young professor who's new to town. Poor bastard doesn't even know what he's getting himself into.

"Congrats on the new house. I had no idea."

"It was supposed to be a surprise for Hanna. I thought we could rent out our apartments and live together. I was going to take her there today, but then Nate showed up last night and I decided to wait."

"Understandable."

"I need a big favor," I admit.

"Anything."

"Hanna wasn't the only reason I decided to get the house." And I hate this. William has been my best friend for most of my life, and I've prided myself on never taking advantage of his generosity. "I'm talking to a lawyer about pursuing physical custody of Claire. I'm sick of her using my daughter to manipulate me, and I can't stand the thought that she could take her away from me."

"Of course. That's wise. And you need money for the lawyer?"

"I have an offer for the club. Someone who's willing to buy it."

Will leans back in the booth and shakes his head. "Don't be stupid, man. This is your future. Let me lend you money."

I take a breath. Borrowing money from Will would make me feel even worse than this. I don't want it to come to that. "Remember when I was looking into opening the club and you offered to buy in?"

"Sure." His brows shoot up, disappearing under his messy mop of blond curls. "Are you saying I can buy in now?"

"If you're interested. It would take a lot of pressure off, but I don't want you to feel pressured."

"Don't even think about it. This is important, and I'd love to do it. What does Hanna think about the custody situation?"

I release a slow a breath. "I didn't want to bring it up until I knew I could do it. We'll have three babies under the age of one. Am I crazy?"

"Fucking nuts," Will says. "But would you have it any other way?"

I grin. "Not a chance."

NATE

I didn't want to leave Asher's until I was sure Collin was asleep, and by the time I make it to the dock, Hanna's already there. She's sitting against the railing, looking out over the water. Her dark hair is off her neck in a twist, and my fingers itch to toy with the little tendrils that have escaped. I miss the way her hair feels, miss the way her eyes float closed as I comb it with my fingers.

The night is clear and the moon reflects off her pale skin, and looking at her hurts so much that I wonder for a few breathless seconds if I can breathe near her, knowing she's not mine.

"It's a beautiful night." I consider sinking onto the planks next to her but dismiss the idea. I don't trust myself to be that close. I take my station on the other side of the dock instead.

"It is." She stands and crosses to stand next to me. Her smell slingshots me back to weekends waking up in hotels with Hanna's hair fanned across the pillow, her soft curves under my hands.

"Why are we here?" If the question comes out harsher than I intended, it's because I'm desperate to get away.

She reaches in her purse and hands me a folded piece of paper. "Because I need to tell you about this."

I unfold the paper and my hammering heart is blindsided by the black-and-white image. I can barely make it out in the moonlight, but I know what it is.

"Mine?" My voice breaks on the word.

"They don't have to be," she whispers.

I rip my gaze away from the ultrasound image to see her face. "What's that supposed to mean?"

"I'm telling you because it's the right thing to do. But I'm not asking anything of you. I wouldn't do that."

"You think I'd just walk away from my child?"

"Children." She points to two spots on the image. One gray lima bean and the other.

My breath is trapped in my lungs, and I have to close my eyes to remember how to breathe. "Children?" When I open my eyes again, she's staring at me, trying to read my expression.

Finally, she nods. "Twins."

My stomach feels like it's stuck in an endless free fall as I study the little, colorless splotches in the moonlight. Twins. *My* twins.

"Does Max know?"

"Yes."

"He knows they're mine?"

A breeze picks up off the river, and a wispy lock of hair blows across her face. "Yes."

"When are you getting married? Wasn't that supposed to be soon?"

She shakes her head. "We called off the wedding. Postponed it indefinitely. I can't move forward with anything like that until after the babies are born. Right now, they're my only priority."

"And then?"

She shrugs. "We're engaged. I plan to marry him eventually. Just not yet."

"Do you expect me to just walk away? Let you two create your happy little family with my children?" Hanna is one of three people in the world who could understand how much that hurts me. Yet here we are. Here I am—on the outside again.

"I don't know what to expect from you. I just know the choice needs to be yours, and that's why I'm telling you."

My whole body tenses and an ugly laugh slips from my lips. "My choice? What if my choice is to be in their lives every day? What if my choice is to have them in my house? What if I want to be a real father and not just someone they visit from time to time? Are you giving me that choice?"

"You are their father, and I won't keep them from you. But I am their mother. If you fight me for custody"—she lifts her eyes to mine and I see her determination—"I will fight back just as hard. You will lose."

"What if I don't just fight for my kids?" I ask. Vivian says I keep walls around my heart, but I would take a sledgehammer to those walls for Hanna. I would tear them down and stand completely exposed, all to get closer to her. "What if I fight for their mother too?"

HANNA

Will I ever be able to look at Nate and not feel this painful tugging in my heart?

"Didn't you already have your chance?" My fingernails bite into my palms as I force my hands to stay at my sides.

"I couldn't fight for you before."

I draw in a breath, and he opens his eyes to meet mine. The question I can't ask pulses in the air between us. *Why not?*

"What if I won, Hanna? What if I fought for you and I won? I'm not the prize here. *You* are." He turns then, reaches out, and his fingers stroke the side of my cheek. My eyes float closed because it's too much—having him here when he's supposed to be dead, having him touch me when I'm supposed to let him go. "It would be different if you hadn't chosen him, if you weren't in love with him." His fingers take my chin and tilt it up until I open my eyes and look into his. "It would be different if I didn't know that you're too damn good for me. I came here, and you had made your choice and forgotten me. I knew I didn't deserve your heart, and I didn't want to risk breaking it."

I step back until his hand falls away from my face. "Too late."

"That's why you chose him? Because I didn't fight for you? Come to LA with me. Be with me. I will fight for you every day."

"Would you even say that if you didn't know about the pregnancy?" My voice is cold even to my own ears. Instinctively, my hand splays over my stomach, where my babies grow. According to all the pregnancy websites, today my little ones are no bigger than the size of a kidney bean. Not much. Yet...*everything*.

"I'm supposed to be dead." He squeezes my hand when I try to pull away. "As soon as we arrived in Afghanistan, I realized I couldn't do the tour. I was a mess. I needed some time alone, so I went to India to join Janelle and left my agent behind with the other musicians..." He closes his eyes. "I should have been on that helicopter and I should be dead right now, and the only reason I'm alive is because I'm so fucking in love with you that I couldn't face my tour. Don't you see? You save me. Over and over again."

I lick my lips and taste the salt of my tears. Maybe I'll always love Nate, and maybe that love for Nate will destroy what I have with Max. But this isn't about Max. This isn't as simple as choosing between two men. I'm not willing to move to LA, and I won't ask him to leave Collin to be here. I love him enough to let him go.

I understand the difference now. I'm not walking away from him. I'm letting him go.

"I want to go to your next appointment," he says. "I'm their father. I want to be part of this."

"Okay."

"But do me a favor. Don't bring him with you."

I take a breath. "If I marry him, he'll be helping me raise them, regardless of how you feel about that."

His gaze settles on my left hand. "*If?*"

"*When*," I whisper, but the word feels like a lie.

FIVE

MAX

When I hear the click of the shower door opening and closing, I get hard instantly. Because the thought of Hanna joining me in my shower does that to me.

I haven't touched her since Nate appeared on her doorstep Friday night. I called her last night after she met with Nate, but her mind was somewhere else. I wanted to go to her apartment, to hold her and reassure us both, but I didn't want to push her when I knew she was emotional and confused.

"Want company?" she whispers.

As I turn to her, I'm already filled with thoughts of pressing her against the tile as I kiss her. I want to remind her how it feels when we're together. I want to sink to my knees so I can put my mouth between her legs as the hot water spills over her.

When I wipe the water from my face, I freeze. "What the fuck?"

Meredith skims her eyes over me, all the way down to my cock, and grins. "Good morning." She reaches for me, and I shove her aside and leave the shower.

Hanna's supposed to meet me here so we can head over to brunch at her mom's together. It's become our Sunday routine—as Meredith well knows, since she's met us here on the last two

Sundays to hand off Claire. No doubt she hoped Hanna would find us together, wet from the shower.

I wrap a towel around my hips and storm from the bathroom, determined to put distance between Meredith and me before I do something I regret.

I have my jeans on by the time she joins me in the bedroom.

"That didn't turn out how I was hoping," she grumbles, plopping her nude, wet body onto my bed.

I throw my towel over her. "Was that supposed to be sexy? Did you think you could climb into the shower with me and I wouldn't be able to resist you?"

Her lower lip sticks out in a pout, and she removes the towel and uses it to dry her hair. "I thought maybe you could use some cheering up."

"Would you just stop for a minute and imagine if our roles were reversed? If I were trying to reconcile with you and got naked and joined you in the shower?"

"I'd be down for that."

Feeling her eyes on me literally makes me sick to my stomach. "If *you* do it, it's supposed to be sexy, but you know what it would be called if a guy did it to you?"

Her eyes go hard and her nostrils flare. "What?"

"Assault, Meredith. I'm going to say one more time that I'm not interested. I want you to stay away from me. This shit isn't sexy and it doesn't turn me on. It's sad and pathetic." I tug on a shirt.

"Her baby daddy is alive, Max. You're living in a fantasy world if you think she's going to marry you when she could have him."

I force myself to take a breath before I talk. "Are you listening? I need you to hear this. Whatever Hanna decides—whether she marries me or Nate Crane or the fucking man in the moon—I will never, ever be with you again. I would rather be alone than be with you. I would rather be abstinent for the rest of my life than have you in my bed. I tolerate you because you're my daughter's mother. That's it and that's all, and the next time you enter my house without my express permission, I'll call the police and have them drag your delusional ass to jail. Do I make myself clear?" I leave the bedroom before she can answer.

Hanna's waiting for me in the living room, her eyes wide.

Of course. *Fuck.*

"Hanna, I can exp—"

"I heard. All of it. She's lost her mind."

My shoulders sag with relief and I gather her into my arms. "She's never known how to be alone. But this is a new low. I think..." I take a breath and slowly let it out.

Meredith has always been one to go after what she wants, and she never paid much mind to anyone who stood in her way, but it's been different since Claire was born. More desperate.

"Would you quit talking about me?" Meredith emerges from the bedroom, fully dressed, her hair hanging in wet clumps around her shoulders. She narrows her eyes at Hanna. "How's Nate?"

"Alive," Hanna says dryly.

"So I hear. Have you even told Max about your fun little trips this summer? All over the fucking country. Or should I say, all over the country, *fucking*?"

"Did you need something?" Hanna asks her, and I'm proud of her. Six months ago, Meredith would have had Hanna turning away to hide in a corner. She's changed. She's stronger now, more confident. Did I do that, or was it Nate?

"Fine," Meredith says. "I'm out. Where's Claire?"

"She's napping." I nod to the Pack 'N Play on the other side of the room. "I'll bring her by your place later."

"Fine."

"I need to tell you something," I say when we're alone.

Her teeth sink into her bottom lip. "Okay?"

"I'm getting a lawyer and pursing custody of Claire. I know it seems crazy with the twins coming, and I hope you understand—"

"I think it's wonderful." Her face lights up with her grin. "You're an amazing father, and I hope you win."

I release a breath and tension I hadn't realized I felt dissolves from my shoulder. "Thank you," I whisper, "for understanding."

She splays her fingers over her belly. "I understand more than you know," she says with a sad smile.

"How are you holding up? Did it go okay with Nate last night?"

She stiffens at his name. "He asked me to move to LA."

Of course he did. "And what did you say?"

She blinks at me. "I'm not leaving New Hope. This is my home."

"He wanted more than for you to move to LA." I take a step closer. I need to touch her. I wonder if she knows she's pulling away from me, if she can feel it like I can. It's as if we're connected by a thousand little threads like those in a woven rug and they've been breaking one at a time since the moment Nate came back into town. With every breath, I feel another thread snap. "He wanted *you*."

She shrugs. "I'm already taken."

I draw in a deep breath. She lifts her hand to my face and skims her fingers along my jaw.

I groan softly and slide my hand into her hair as I lower my mouth to hers. She's soft and sweet, and I need more of her.

Taking a fistful of her skirt, I yank her dress up around her waist and find the cotton of her panties. She gasps, and I rub her through the fabric as her fingers curl into my back. My lips find her neck and the skin in the sensitive juncture of neck and shoulder.

"Max," she says. But it's not the normal breathy, needy whispering of my name. The word is a warning. A yield sign. "Max."

My hand stills and I pull back to look into her eyes. I'm blindsided by the apology I see there. "Let's move in together."

"What?" She blinks at me. If she's thinking I have the world's worst timing with important proposals, she's not wrong.

"We could rent out our apartments and use the money to rent a little place together. Someplace without those stairs that scare the living shit out of me every time I think of you climbing them. Someplace we can make our own." I take her hand and squeeze. "You didn't want to move in together last spring because you knew your mom would flip if you lived with a guy before marriage, but we're not trying to maintain appearances anymore, are we?" She looks at the floor, and I tilt her chin back up so her eyes meet mine. "I could give two shits about appearances. I want to wake up with you in my arms, Hanna. I want to know I'm going to be right there when you need me, every time you need me. You and Claire are all that matter in my world. I want everything that matters to be what

I come home to every night."

"I'm sorry." She steps back. "I just can't. I'm too confused right now."

My lungs burn as I fill them—it hurts to breathe in a world where Hanna isn't mine.

"I know it's not fair. And I want a future with you, but..."

"But you can't stop thinking about him."

"I can't move in with you right now," she says softly. "That wouldn't be fair to either of us. It's not that simple."

"You keep saying that."

I swallow back the rest of what I want to say right along with my anger, frustration, and the betrayal I've never allowed myself to feel. While I was waiting for her to take my ring, she was with another man, and I was never allowed to be angry because that man died and she needed to grieve.

I drag a hand through my hair and look at the ceiling. "Was it that simple when you made love to him?"

"Can we not do this?"

Torment is etched across her face, and I can't stand to know I'm the one who put it there. I pull her against my chest.

"I won't rush you, but remember something for me," I whisper into her hair. "You put on my ring."

NATE

Collin tosses the stones into the river and claps when each splashes into the water.

But fuck if my stomach doesn't pitch every time I think of Hanna and Max having a life together, laughing together, in bed together. Raising my children together.

"Hey, sexy," a tall blonde murmurs from behind her stroller. And I'll give her credit—it takes one hell of a lot of self-confidence to try to play the slut while walking your infant through the park.

I turn away, silently dismissing her.

"We have mutual friends." She parks the stroller and sinks onto the bench beside me, but not before giving me an obvious once-over. "Congratulations on the whole avoiding-a-fiery-death thing."

"Thanks," I reply dryly. I keep my eye on Collin.

"So you're in New Hope for a while, probably hoping to win Hanna back, huh?"

My jaw tightens. "I don't know what you're talking about." Then I stand because I'm not in the mood.

"Oh," she calls to my back. "Because the rest of the town seems to think those are your babies she's carrying."

I stop and slowly turn to her, and I can tell by her face that she expected this to be news to me. "I don't know who you think you are or why you think I care about your opinions about my private business, but you're mistaken. You can leave now."

She attempts to look innocent and adjusts her baby's blanket. "Twins—can you believe it? Surely you're going to want to be in those babies' lives, though, right? I mean, it won't be easy now that they're moving in together, but I bet you and Hanna have worked something out."

My stomach clenches, and surprise must show on my face because she smiles—slow and wide. It reminds me of the hyenas in the Disney movie Collin loves to watch. She finally hit her mark.

"Who are you?" I ask.

"I'm a friend who wants to see everyone get what they deserve. Nothing less. Nothing more."

MAX

Hanna's mother beams as she opens the door for me. "So glad you could make it for brunch."

"Thanks for inviting me, Gretchen."

"We missed you at church." She turns to the living room. "Hanna, Max is here."

Hanna pushes off the couch to greet me with a kiss on my cheek.

"Hi," she says. "How was your morning? Post-crazy-baby-mama drama?"

"Good." I spent it in my office at the club, trying to work magic with numbers and not succeeding. "How was church?"

She shrugs. "Mom is worried for the souls of her sinner daughters. We like to throw her a bone once in a while."

"Food is ready!" her mom calls. "Everyone in the dining room, please!"

We file into the dining room behind Gretchen—Granny, Liz, Abby, Hanna, Maggie, Asher, me, and a couple of Gretchen's friends—and line up at the buffet to fill our plates.

Gretchen takes Hanna's plate from her before she can fill it. "I want you to try this new recipe."

Liz and Hanna gape as their mother heaps hash brown casserole onto Hanna's plate. The potatoes are bubbling with cheese and butter.

"The baby needs the calcium," Gretchen says.

"I think hell just froze over," Liz mumbles, and her mom shoots her a stern glare.

When our plates are full, we find our seats around the table.

"Liz," Gretchen says, "I thought you might bring that nice gentleman you danced with at Will and Cally's wedding. That friend of yours… Max, what's his name? Sam something or other."

"You don't want me bringing Sam Bradshaw to a family brunch," Liz says next to me, scowling at her food.

"Why not?" her mother objects.

Hanna bites back a smile.

"He really likes you, Liz," I tell her, not for the first time.

"You're blushing!" their little sister Abby says. "You never blush!"

"It's hot in here," Liz grumbles.

Across from me, Maggie moans softly. "These potatoes. Oh my God! Mom, I had no idea you had it in you."

"She let me cook today," Granny says. "That's how food is supposed to taste."

My phone vibrates in my pocket and I pull it out to see a message from Meredith. *Can you come get Claire? A client has an emergency.*

"A haircut emergency?" Liz says, shamelessly reading from my phone. "Whatever."

Who knows if it's true or if Meredith just knows that this is my time with Hanna's family.

"My apologies, Gretchen." I stand and slide my phone back into my pocket. "I need to get my daughter. Her mother has to work."

Hanna stands. "I'll give you a call later."

I'll give you a call. Not, *I'll see you.*

She kisses me on the cheek, and I stop her before she can pull away. I press my mouth to hers. It's not a long kiss or a passionate one—her family is right here—but it's firm and sure and right. It's everything my love for her is.

SIX

NATE

I scratch out the last four lines on the page, pushing the pen so deep it cuts through the paper. I'm working on this collaboration with Asher and I'm stuck on the ballad.

All week, all I've been able to think about is Hanna moving in with Max, Hanna waking up next to Max, Hanna raising my babies *with Max.*

It's a good thing Collin is here. Otherwise, I probably would have already left Asher's in favor of getting trashed in a hotel room somewhere.

I stare at the marked-out lyrics and then throw the notebook across the room.

"What did that notebook ever do to you?"

I'm probably scowling when I look up at Maggie, but scowling is pretty tame considering how I'm feeling right now. How I've felt all week.

"She's having my babies and she's marrying him." I can tell by her face that this isn't news to her. Fuck. Of course not. "What am I supposed to do with that?"

She plops into a chair across from me and folds her legs under herself. "Asher told me that he warned you to stay away from her."

"I don't need a lecture tonight, Maggie."

"Asher also told me that ignoring a friend's wishes for a girl wasn't like you. But something about Hanna made you do it anyway."

I lean my head back and look at the ceiling, remembering that night, remembering her body moving against mine as we danced, the pitch in her voice when she asked me to kiss her. "She's my kryptonite."

"You're such a dork."

"Are they really moving in together?"

Maggie frowns. "Isn't that what people do when they get married?"

But Hanna said she wasn't moving forward until after the babies were born, and I hoped that meant… "Does she really love him?"

She picks at the seam of her jeans, and just when I think she's going to avoid answering the question altogether, she says, "I don't know Hanna as well as Liz does, so maybe I'm not the one to ask, but she's going through a really hard time right now. She spent her whole life believing she was undesirable because no one noticed her, and no one noticed her because she hid in the shadows, and she hid in the shadows because she didn't think anyone would want her." She lifts her eyes to mine. She's trying to read me. To decide if I'm worth her interpretation of the truth. To decide if I'm worthy of Hanna.

"What does all of that have to do with Max? With me?"

Maggie shakes her head and gives a sardonic smile. "Men," she mutters. "Of course you don't get it."

"Enlighten me."

"She doesn't even know who she is anymore. Her whole perception of herself has been blown to pieces because now two great guys want her. And to answer your question? Yes. She loves him."

I tear my eyes away from her and grab my guitar because I need something to do with my hands.

"She loves you too. You know that. You can't tell me you can spend two seconds around her without feeling it."

"But?"

Maggie shrugs. "The choice isn't mine."

I strum a chord on the guitar—the opening chord to the song with the elusive lyrics. In my mind, it's always been "Hanna's song," but I never called it that. The first chord, then the second.

"I never believed she'd choose him," I say softly. "Maybe I didn't realize it at the time, but in retrospect, I know I thought I was the easy choice."

"Why?"

"Because she fits me. Because life was this crazy, chaotic disappointment and then Hanna came along and everything got quiet. Everything slowed down. It's like I spent my whole life only half filling my lungs because I was too busy running to the next thing. She makes me take a deep breath. She silences the bullshit and washes away my ambivalence." I drag a hand through my hair. "And I assumed that I did all of that for her too."

Maggie studies me for a quiet minute. "You're not so bad, Nate Crane."

"I'm a fuck-up," I mutter. "A fuck-up who can't keep his promise."

"What promise is that?"

"I promised that, if she chose him, I'd let her go. I promised that I wouldn't make her second-guess her decision."

"You think you broke that promise?"

I shake my head, grinning now. "No. But I plan to."

HANNA

"Somebody had a late night," I call when Liz pushes into the bakery.

She looks like hell warmed over this morning. Her blond curls are pulled back in a ponytail and her eyes are barely open. And thank God she's here. Mom showed up twenty minutes ago and has been quizzing me about my plans for the twins. It's not even seven a.m. and my brain is spinning with information on breastfeeding and the dangers of co-sleeping as well as her opinions about the attachment parenting movement.

"It's not the late night that's the problem," Liz mutters. "It's the early morning."

Mom frowns at her and clears her throat. "Claudia Bauer saw you leaving Sam Bradshaw's apartment the other day. Sam's a nice boy, but if you give him what he wants now, he's never going to marry you."

Liz narrows her puffy eyes at Mom. "I don't want to marry Sam," she growls, heading for the coffee. "I just want to fuck him."

Mom gasps, and I have to bite my lip to keep from laughing. Seriously, the woman should know better than to pick a fight with Liz this early in the morning. Liz and mornings are mortal enemies, and she takes her loathing out on everyone stupid enough to get too close.

Mom huffs. "I'll say an extra prayer for you at church, Elizabeth. Your sister Maggie went through this phase too. And now Hanna's having babies out of wedlock. Heaven help me, you'd think I didn't bring my girls up in the Church."

Liz mutters something unintelligible under her breath. Probably for the best that Mom couldn't hear.

I pack up an assortment of pastries and see Mom to the door. "Take these for your Bible study group," I say. When she's gone, I turn to Liz. "I cannot believe you just told our mother you were using Sam Bradshaw for sex."

She chugs half her cup of creamer-and-sugar-filled coffee before replying. "I didn't say I was using him for sex. I said I don't want to marry him. I want to fuck him. And the look on her face was totally worth it."

"You're going to burn in hell." I giggle.

"Well, I'll have the best company." She laughs, but then her face goes serious again. "I have to tell you something."

"I don't know if I like the sound of that."

Sighing, she avoids my gaze. "You know how much I appreciate my job, don't you? I mean, you took me in and gave me work when you were pissed at me for the whole Max thing. Even though I totally wish you would have *told* me that's why you were pissed, I still think it's pretty awesome that you did that for me."

"Are you quitting?"

"Yeah," she says. "Kind of. Do you hate me?"

"Of course not! Did you get a new job? That's great!" I hug her, and when I draw back, she's grinning.

"I'm so excited. One of the girls who graduated from the El Ed program with me is starting a preschool, and she wants me to be her partner. Isn't that awesome?"

"Oh, Liz! That's great! I'm so happy for you!"

She frowns. "But you already work too much, and now that you're pregnant, I really hate leaving."

"Don't worry about it," I insist. "I never intended to have you here forever. You were helping me with my dream, and now it's time for you to go after yours."

"Best. Sister. Ever," she whispers.

"Just tell me what I can do to help."

"How about you start by planning to enroll those babies of yours in my preschool when the time comes. I'll hold their spot."

I feel the blood drain from my face. "I never realized how many decisions and plans are required when you're a new mother. It's just overwhelming. I know I won't be doing it alone, and I know Max would help me with anything I wanted, but I feel guilty because it's all I ever talk about and they're not even his babies." I take a breath and then another. Then I go to the kitchen to get a cold washcloth for my face because that's the best thing I've found for these nausea spells.

Liz follows me and beats me to the sink, wetting a towel and handing it to me.

The bell in the front rings, letting us know someone just arrived.

"I'll get it," she says.

"Thanks." I drape the washcloth across my forehead and close my eyes, listening to Liz talk to the customer.

"Oh," she says. "Hmm. Um. How are you?"

"Where's Hanna?" I know the voice, and an unwelcome thrill dances up my spine as Nate pushes into my kitchen and stalks toward me.

"Customers aren't allowed back here," Liz says behind him.

"Don't do it," he says, and those dark, broody eyes are all over me like he's trying to take me in, memorize me.

I take a deep breath and look to my sister. "You should probably go." Then I turn to Nate. "Don't do what?"

"Um…" Liz looks Nate up and down. "Are you sure? Because I can stay to protect you. Or…try." God bless her, she's standing behind Nate with her hands on her hips, ready to swing on my behalf.

"Why don't you give us a minute?"

She narrows her eyes at Nate. "Hurt her and I'll cut off your balls in your sleep." Then she pushes out of the kitchen, the door swinging wildly behind her.

"Don't move in with him," Nate says.

"What are you talking about?" I ask.

"I thought you said you weren't moving forward with Max until after the babies were born. Don't you think moving in is moving forward?"

"I don't know where you get your information, but I'm not moving in with him."

"You're not?"

I shake my head. "He asked me to, and I said no."

He must have been expecting a fight, because his shoulders relax and he drags a hand through his hair. "Thank you."

I toss my washcloth into the sink. "Is that all?"

"No." He lifts his eyes to mine. "I need to apologize."

"For what?"

"For this."

In two long strides, he closes the space between us and presses his mouth to mine. His lips are hot and hungry as his tongue sweeps inside—coaxing and demanding all at once. And it's so good. So sweet and easy and safe that, for a breath, I forget how wrong it is. I'm back in the hotel in St. Louis, finding myself in the fire between us. For a breath, I forget that I'm wearing Max's ring.

I shove at his shoulder and push him away. "Don't do that again." My stomach squeezes, and my heart is so battered and beaten that it's unrecognizable.

NATE

Her eyes flash with anger, disappointment, and heat. "Do you think you can win me with a kiss? Did you think I'm so fickle that your mouth on mine is enough to convince me to break Max's heart?"

I step forward, blocking her between me and the counter as I lower my mouth to her ear. "I thought maybe you needed a reminder."

"What do you want from me? You want me to admit that I want you? You know I do. You want me to tell you I'm still in love with you? It's true."

My heart swells and hammers at her words. I don't know if I'll ever feel worthy of Hanna's love, but that doesn't change that I want it, *need* it like I need air.

"Isn't that enough? Is it like this with him? When he's whispering in your ear, does your body hum with need? We both know I could kiss you again and make you forget him. I could kiss you until you wanted me so badly you climbed onto that counter and let me touch you everywhere, let me do anything I wanted with your body."

"You won't," she says, her voice shaking slightly.

"Are you so sure?"

"You won't," she repeats, "because I'm asking you not to. You won't because you're too good not to respect that."

"I don't want to be *good*," I growl. I step back so I can see her face—her parted lips, her smoky eyes. "I want *you*."

"I'm taken."

"What happened?" I ask, scanning her face, trying to read her shielding expression. "Between when I left LA and when I came back to New Hope, what happened to make you take him back?"

She's silent for a minute, and I wonder if she's going to tell me the truth. "I found out he bought me the bakery—that all my worries and insecurities about our relationship were totally unfounded."

"I'll buy you a hundred bakeries."

"But I don't want a hundred bakeries. I only want this one."

Here. In New Hope. I close my eyes because I can't deny that geography still stands between us.

"Please don't kiss me again."

"What if you ask me to?"

She swallows. "I won't ask."

SEVEN

HANNA

The wind is cool as it rolls off the river and through the changing leaves. Autumn in New Hope has to be one of the most beautiful things I've ever seen. The leaves turn orange, red, brown, even purple, fall from the trees, and float by on the river. I'll always associate the sound of leaves crunching underfoot with my childhood, with home.

But today, it doesn't bring me the comfort I need. My conversation with Nate demands too much of my attention for anything to comfort me.

"Between when I left LA and when I came back to New Hope, what happened to make you take him back?"

You died. They were the words I didn't say, but they've been there, in my mind and on my tongue, since he asked the question. Are they true? Did I only go back to Max because I thought Nate was dead?

"How are you holding up?"

I look up to see Maggie pulling a chair up to the patio set behind William's art gallery. She asked me to meet her here, and something about my carefree sister scheduling a conversation has left butterflies in my stomach.

"I'm okay," I answer. "Emotional, but I blame the hormones."

"Yeah," she says, "not the fact that you're in love with two men, wearing one's ring, and carrying the other's babies?"

"Well, that sums it up rather nicely." I've been trying to convince myself that nothing between Max and me has changed, but I don't invite him to stay over anymore, and every time he kisses me, I feel ashamed and confused.

"Sorry." She shrugs. "I know something about loving two men at once. Listen," she says after studying me for a minute. "Before you dig your heels in about staying with Max, I want you to think about it."

I stiffen. I know Maggie loves me and has my best interests at heart, but after today, when I can still feel Nate's lips press against mine, when his scent lingers on my skin, this is the last thing I need.

"I have thought about it, and I made my decision—weeks ago, before the accident. I put on his ring."

"I'm saying don't blindly trust a decision you can't remember making. Ask yourself if you would choose Max again today—at this very moment—if you had to make your decision again."

"I don't know." If I'd known that my night with Nate left me pregnant, who knows what my choice would have been? "No matter what I do, someone gets hurt."

"Stop trying to figure out why you made the choice then and start trying to figure out what choice is right for you now. You're trying to protect Max, and as much as he wants to marry you, I don't think that's where he would want your decision to come from."

"I don't want to hurt him," I whisper. "He's too good. He doesn't deserve to be hurt."

"I know, sweetie."

I watch a young couple jog by along the river. "How did you know? When you decided to be with Asher, to move in with him, how did you know it was the right decision?"

"Hanna." She waits until I look at her. "I knew because I didn't have to ask myself if I was making the right decision. When I was engaged to Will, I kept asking myself over and over again if I was doing the right thing. I would mentally tally all the reasons I should marry him and feel guilty for questioning it, and then the next day, the next hour, sometimes even the next minute, I'd do it all over again. But that should have been my first hint." She smiles then takes my hands in hers. "I know you're a grown woman and you have your head on your shoulders better than I probably ever will, so it seems ridiculous for me to give you advice, but I'm going to anyway. Give Max his ring back."

"Maggie—"

"Hear me out. Please?"

"Okay." But my stomach twists into a painful knot because I'm scared that I won't want to hear what she has to say.

"Maybe you're meant to be with Max. Maybe you two will work this out and you'll have these babies and find that all you want is to spend your life with Max at your side. Maybe there will come a day that he'll tell you all he needs is you and you'll be as sure as I am with Asher." She cocks her head and gives me a sad smile. "But, sweetie, it's all over your face that you're not there now. I'm not saying this because I'm Nate's friend and trying to give him a foot-up. I'm saying this because you're my sister and I love you, and I refuse to see you make the mistake that Krystal and I almost made. You owe it to yourself and to Max to give back that ring until you know for sure what you want."

A tear splashes onto the glass tabletop, and I stand up and walk down the stairs to the lawn. Maggie's not telling me anything I don't already know. But I've been putting off the inevitable.

Maggie wraps an arm around me. I lean my head against her shoulder as she smooths my hair and we watch the wind play in the leaves and the blue evening sky turn to the pink and orange of the setting sun.

It's been ten hours since the kiss, but when I open the door to meet Max at his new rental house, I can still feel the pressure of Nate's lips against mine. I can still smell his clean scent as if it's been branded to my clothing.

The house is nice. Nothing fancy, but it's clean and functional. The table is set, the candles are lit, and the wine is chilling in a bucket of ice on the island.

Max is at the stove, cooking dinner, with Claire strapped to his chest in a baby carrier. He's humming softly as he stirs chicken and vegetables in a sauté pan, and Claire's eyes open and float closed again and again.

I'm slammed with a vision of our future together, raising Claire and the twins side by side. Max is the kind of guy who would treat them all as his own, and he'll be the kind of husband who cooks dinner when I have to work late or just because. I'll have my bakery and he'll have his health club. Once we're married, I'll have access to my trust fund, so money won't be so tight, and even if it were, we'd make it work. He'd hold my hand when I worried about something, kiss my forehead and reassure me. He'll be an amazing husband and father. Everything I could have ever wanted or dreamed.

But he'll never be Nate Crane, and every day we're together, I will hate myself for being so completely and painfully aware of that.

Max shouldn't have to be Nate. Because he's an amazing and wonderful guy just as he is.

I press my hand to my lips and stumble back a few steps because things could have been different. If I'd figured out how to accept myself, my body, before he asked me out, they *would* have been different. I'd be looking at a future with an amazing man holding my hand rather than bracing myself for one where I raise my children alone.

Max wouldn't want me to marry him if he knew the decision was motivated by my desire to protect him.

He takes the pan off the stove and turns to pour its contents into a bowl on the island. When he spots me, his face lights up, and that makes me feel even worse.

Maggie's right. Whatever I decided before the accident and why I made that decision is irrelevant.

MAX

“Let me put her down.” Hanna reaches her arms out for Claire, and I gently remove her from the carrier.

She is going to make an amazing mother. She snuggles Claire against her chest and hums softly as she paces around the living room. The two people in this world I would do anything for. My woman. Holding my daughter.

“Goodnight, Claire,” she whispers, carefully lowering her into the crib in the corner. “You sleep well knowing you have the best daddy ever.”

“Come over here,” I murmur.

She’s in a red, strapless sundress tonight, and the sight of her legs and the bare, soft skin of her shoulders is slowly making me lose my mind.

She scans the table and then meets my eyes as the music kicks on. “Max…”

“I wanted to do something nice for you.” I take her hands and squeeze her fingers. “Someday, I’ll be able to take you to fancy restaurants in Indianapolis and Chicago instead of cooking for you. Someday, I’ll be able to buy you the kind of gifts you deserve and surprise you with weekends away at luxurious spas. You deserve it, and I’ll make it happen.”

She closes her eyes, and I count the beats of my anxious heart as I wait. “I don’t care about all that.”

“I love you, Hanna. I just want you to wake up every day and know—without a doubt in your mind—that you’re engaged to a man who loves you and wants to make up for being blind for so many years.”

“I’ve loved you since I was thirteen.” She removes her hands from mine, and the first prickling of dread starts its ominous crawl toward my heart. “And I still think you’re one of the best men I have ever met.”

“Hanna.” We both know where this is going. “What happened?”

Her eyes fill with new tears, and I see what’s coming all over her face. I've seen it coming all week.

"Don't do this."

"I have to." She puts her hand to the side of my face then drops it quickly, as if touching me costs her. "You loved me and sacrificed for me—you knew the bakery was my dream and you went to extraordinary measures to make sure I got it. I'll pay you back and I'll never forget."

My lungs are tight and I can't make them take air. "You changed the way I see the world. You made me see what love could be. The bakery is nothing compared to that. I would do anything for you."

"I know," she says, and fat tears roll down her cheeks. "And don't you think it's time that goes both ways?"

"Don't."

"You deserve better than me."

I want to object. To tell her she's so wrong—that a future with her in any form is better than I deserve—but my throat is thick with emotion and there's no room for words.

She tilts her head to the side, and more tears stream from her eyes as she pulls my grandmother's ring from her finger. She may as well be ripping out my heart.

She takes my hand and presses the ring into my palm. "I can't be with you when my heart's not mine to give, and I won't ask you to wait for me anymore."

"Are you leaving me for him? Is he going to give you a future? Commitment? Raise the babies by your side?"

She shakes her head. "This isn't about him. New Hope is my home, and LA is his. I'm not going anywhere."

I can't help myself anymore, and I gather her into my arms, pulling her against my chest. "Don't do this. I know you don't remember, but you chose me. There was a reason you chose me."

She lets me hold her for a few breaths, and I can feel her tears soaking through the cotton of my shirt. I breathe in her scent, and when I pull away, regret is all over her face.

"I never wanted to hurt you," she says, her eyes moist.

I want to kiss her. Hold her. Beg her to reconsider.

"I need to leave," she whispers. "I'm so sorry."

My grandmother's ring bites into my palm as I watch her head out the door.

EIGHT

HANNA

Four Days Before Hanna's Accident

When I knock on Max's door, it occurs to me that this is probably a terrible place to do this. I could have waited until tomorrow morning and caught him at the club. I could have called and asked him to meet me at the bakery. Instead, I came to his apartment.

The last time I was here, I took off my clothes and begged him to have sex with me. The last time I was here, he turned me down.

"Try me. Come back here sober and test me, Hanna."

Ever since I got back from LA, I've been thinking about that night at Max's house. Did I really want him to make love to me, or did I only say that because I knew he wouldn't do it when I'd been drinking? I think part of me meant it at the time. I love Max, and if Meredith hadn't screwed everything up, we'd be on our way to a wedding by now.

And now I'm here to give him back his ring.

When Max pulls the door open, he looks exhausted, but he grins as soon as he sees me. "Hey," he says softly.

"Hey."

He pulls the door wider, his gaze skimming over me. I'm in a jean skirt and red wrap shirt, nothing special, but his eyes on me make me feel beautiful. Sexy. Wanted.

"I don't suppose you're here for the same reason you were last time?"

My heart thuds, stumbles, and trips in my chest, and I can feel my cheeks burn. "I'm afraid not."

He makes some sort of unintelligible sound at the back of his throat then says, "You want to come in?"

"Yeah. I mean, assuming Meredith's not hiding in there somewhere." I regret my joke when his face falls.

"There's nothing between us but Claire."

I follow him into the apartment and notice he has a Pack 'N Play set up in the corner and a diaper bag on the counter. Was all of that there when I was here last week and I was just too drunk to notice?

"I'm pretty sure Meredith wants me to think there's more," I say.

"What did she say to you?"

"She likes to send me texts when she's over here. Implying… things."

Max's fingers are on my chin, tilting my face up until my eyes meet his. "I haven't touched her since before I kissed you for the first time in November."

My gut twists with guilt. Because maybe he hasn't touched anyone else, but I can't say the same. How would he feel if he knew I gave my virginity to another man? That I've been dating someone else all summer?

I shrug and drop my eyes to the ground. It's not that I can't face him. But there's such a fierce intensity in his blue eyes I'm afraid I'll kiss him if I don't look away. I want to remember what his lips feel like on mine before I say goodbye. I want to have his arms curl around me and hold me tight so I can remember all the good days and stamp them into a safe place in my memory.

"I haven't touched any woman but you, and that will remain true as long as my ring waits in your jewelry box."

I press my palm against my thigh and finger the ring in the pocket of my jeans. I'm not here because I'm choosing Nate. After yesterday, I know Nate and I can't be together. He says he loves me, but he's not willing to sacrifice anything to be with me.

I'm here because I can't choose either one of them, and I need to break it off with both.

Max's gaze drops to my mouth and his eyes turn from warm and tender to hot and hungry. "I miss you, Hanna."

"I miss you too."

He traces my bottom lip with his thumb. My eyes float closed and my muscles soften even as my conscience bristles. I can't keep this up much longer.

"I wanted to talk to you about Abby," I say, and my conscience sings, *Coward!*

"Is she okay?"

"Yeah, but she's taken some pretty radical measures trying to stay thin, and I'm worried about her."

He raises a brow. "I know how you feel."

I frown. "You knew about Abby?"

"I'm talking about being worried about you."

"Oh. No, don't worry about me. I'm fine." Or I will be. Catching Abby with those diet pills was a wakeup call for me, and I made an appointment with a psychiatrist in Indianapolis. "I was hoping you'd talk to her. Maybe go through a healthy, balanced diet and exercise plan. That kind of thing?"

"And would you be there to hear my lecture?"

I draw in a shaky breath. "Sure." Our eyes lock for a minute before I say, "I am working on it. I know I haven't been the healthiest role model for her."

A phone starts ringing in the bedroom and Max sighs. "I need to grab that. Don't go anywhere, okay?"

I nod, and he heads to the bedroom to take the call.

His shoulders are so broad, so strong. I know Max would give me everything Nate wouldn't, and it's so tempting to take what he's offering me.

I wander over to his kitchen table and my gaze catches on a piece of mail at the top of the stack. *Smith, Peterson, and Frank Law Offices of Indianapolis.*

I know that law firm. That's the place that's managing the

arrangement with my anonymous investor for the bakery.

What business could Max have with them?

I can hear Max's low murmurs coming from the bedroom. When I slip the papers from the envelope, I don't even feel guilty for snooping—not much, at least—because I already know what I'm going to see. Max's name and the name of my bakery all on the same letter with the lawyer's letterhead.

I don't get to do more than skim the letter before I hear him end the call. I have to shove the papers back into the envelope and drop them to the table.

"Sorry," he says as he emerges from the bedroom. "That was my mom. Her air conditioner is on the fritz again, and I was troubleshooting with her."

"No, not at all. It's fine. No problem. I hope you can fix it." I'm rambling.

He cocks his head to the side. "Are you okay? You look like you've seen a ghost."

"I'm fine." I nod once, twice…six times like I'm a freaking bobblehead. I was so wrong about Max, and everywhere this summer took me, every decision I made, branched from my disbelief that he ever wanted me for anything more than my money.

But there it is, right on his kitchen table: evidence that he wasn't ever after my money. He was sacrificing his own to make my dreams come true. Evidence that I let my insecurities ruin my future with an amazing man.

"Hanna?"

My eyes fill, and I step forward, wrap my arms around his neck, and hug him as I'd hug any friend who I learned had given me such an amazing gift.

Max wraps his arms around me and presses a kiss to my hair. "What's this for?"

"I'm sorry I took you for granted."

He slides his hand along my jaw and tilts my face up to his. "Ditto," he whispers.

Then he skims his lips over mine in a movement that's so gentle and so tender I nearly disintegrate under it. I kiss him back, unsure whether I'm saying goodbye or welcoming something new into my life.

When he pulls back, his eyes are full of questions, but he only asks one. "Stay with me tonight? We don't have to do anything. I just need you in my arms again."

I don't know what I want, but he takes my silence as my answer and his expression changes and becomes guarded. "I'm sorry," I say, and turn to leave.

"I love you," he calls to my back, and I can only nod. I walk out the door, his grandmother's ring still in my pocket.

HANNA

Present Day

"So freaking *good*," I moan. I let the pure, unadulterated pleasure of fine chocolate ripple through my body.

After I left Max's house, I called Liz, who promised she was on her way, but she brought the whole crew, and now Liz, Maggie, Cally, and Nix are all gathered around my kitchen island with drinks—martinis for the three who aren't knocked up and herbal tea for the rest of us—and pounds of those gourmet chocolates Asher buys Maggie when he's in New York.

Liz raided the bakery and brought up an assortment of cookies and pastries, and Nix brought a silly card game that we haven't bothered playing.

Without my having to explain, they all understand how hard it was for me to give Max his ring back.

"So what happens between you and Nate now?" Nix asks.

Liz is shaking up a new batch of chocolate martinis, and Nix raises her glass to signal she wants another.

"Nothing," I say. I cut a piece of the cheese Danish and hand it to Nix. "This is my new recipe. Tell me if it's too sweet."

"What do you mean, *nothing*?" Nix asks before taking a bite. Then, with her mouth half full, she says, "Oh my God. This isn't food. It's an orgasm in your mouth."

When Liz reaches for the rest of the Danish, Cally smacks her hand away and takes it from the plate. "Pregnant ladies get first dibs."

"Nothing?" Maggie asks. "Are you sure?"

"I didn't break it off with Max so I could be with Nate." Though I'm sure Max believes I did. I'm sure everyone in town will think I did, once word gets out.

"What did he say when you told him you were pregnant?" Nix asks.

"He wants me to move to LA."

"What?" Liz squeaks. "Like you're going to totally throw away your business—your *life*—for him?"

"You can't blame him for trying," Maggie says.

"He's only interested because of the babies. When I went to LA and told him I wasn't going to marry Max, Nate still said goodbye. He doesn't want to be with me—not enough to fight for me when it counts." And not enough to figure out a way to make it work that doesn't involve my moving across the country.

"I'm not sure you're being fair, Hanna," Nix says. "When you went to LA, he thought you'd chosen Max before the accident."

Maggie nods. "I think he was trying to let you go since you wanted to be with Max."

"I didn't walk away. I let you go."

Is that what Nate meant? He let me go so I could be with Max?

"I still don't understand why I chose Max," I say quietly, and the admission fills me with guilt. "Don't get me wrong. I don't know how I could have chosen Nate either. It's an impossible choice. My missing memories are leaving me with a lot of unanswered questions. I still have four days of my life that are missing. I wish I knew what happened in those days."

"Have you thought any more about how the accident may have happened?" Nix asks.

Liz tenses. "What do you mean by that?"

Nix just studies me, so finally I say, "Nix thinks my injuries were too severe to be from just a fall. She suspects that some of them were…inflicted intentionally."

"What? By whom?" Liz asks. "How?"

I nod at Nix, silently giving her permission to talk about it, and she takes a breath. "I think maybe there was foul play—a fight with punches thrown, that kind of thing. I'm not excluding the possibility that Hanna took an accidental fall down the stairs, but given the state of her injuries, I suspected there might be more to it than that. Not knowing Max very well, I immediately asked about him."

"We can rule out that possibility," I say softly. "Max would lay down his life for me."

"What about Meredith?" Maggie says. "You were stealing her man."

Cally snorts. "I'm no defender of Meredith, but a fistfight? That doesn't seem her style."

"True," Liz says. "She might break a nail."

"I'm not convinced there was anything more than a fall," I say. "I wasn't eating and I could have passed out and fallen."

"Even if that's true, that doesn't answer the question about how you came to choose Max," Liz says. "I think it's reasonable to want to know, even if you aren't marrying him."

Maggie's frowning into her wine. "Am I the only one who thinks it seems unlikely that Hanna would give her virginity to Nate and, less than a week later, decide to marry someone else?"

"Maybe," I say softly. Nix, who was about to chime in, shuts her mouth. "Maybe I wanted to make love to Nate for the same reasons any woman wants to have sex with a man she loves. I know that might be hard to understand, but I do love them both." I look at my friends' and sisters' faces. "Letting go of either one of them seemed impossible the day Nate told me I needed to make a choice." *It still seems impossible*, but I don't say that aloud.

Liz refills her wine. "Maybe it came down to which guy could give you the future that you want."

"Probably." I thought of that too.

I don't want to leave New Hope for LA or anywhere. How would a real relationship with Nate even work? Would he want me to move to LA or would our life be a series of two- or three-day visits here and there? Him coming to New Hope when he didn't have performances or need to put time in at the studio, me flying out to see him perform when I could get away from the bakery?

"Max looks better on paper," Cally says. "Except for Meredith, of course."

"Maybe Hanna found out about the bakery," Liz suggests. "I mean, the guy sacrificed his house just so she could have her dream."

"I did," I admit, thinking of my most recent memory. "I was at Max's apartment and I saw a letter from the law firm that handles the arrangement with the bakery. But would that be enough to make me choose to marry him?"

Maggie cocks her head. "So you believe you chose Max over Nate before the accident, and you want to know what finally brought you to your final decision."

I nod. "Wouldn't you?"

Liz opens a drawer and removes a pad of paper and a pen. "Okay, let's figure out what we do know." She writes *HANNA'S MISSING DAYS* at the top and draws a line under it. Down the side, she writes the days of the week through Thursday, and next to Thursday, she writes *Accident on stairs.*

"Can we assume that's when I put on the ring too?" I ask. "Did anyone see it on me before that?"

Liz shakes her head. "That was the day. I would have noticed if you'd had it on sooner." She adds *Puts on ring* to Thursday.

"When did you sleep with Nate?" Maggie asks.

"Saturday," I say, pointing. "And that's when he told me I had to make a choice. Then, later, we..." I swallow. "We got caught up in the moment and had unprotected sex in the shower."

"And hello, twins," Nix says.

"Hello, horribly timed baby conversation," I reply. The girls all stare at me expectantly, so I explain, "It's a new memory. And not a good one."

"How can shower sex with Nate Crane be a *bad* memory?" Nix asks.

My cheeks burn. "Well, *that* part isn't bad."

"I hate you a little right now," Nix says.

"It was the after," I say, "when we realized what we'd done and I..." I swallow hard. "I pushed him about what would happen if I got pregnant, and we had this terrible fight because he didn't want to talk about it and I insisted. I needed to know."

"Of course you did," Liz says. "And you were right to ask."

"I guess," I say. "But think about it from Nate's point of view. He's been commitment-averse since his son was born. He didn't want a long-term relationship, marriage, kids, none of that. Collin comes first. Then, just hours after he said that he'd change his rules *for me*, that he'd find a way to make it work for me, there I am, talking about babies and the future."

"Not for nothing," Maggie says, eyes dropping meaningfully to my stomach. "Turns out it was a conversation you needed to have."

Liz writes *Baby fight* on the chart. "What else?"

I shrug. "I remember going to Max's and finding out about the bakery and then waking up in the hospital."

Cally leans forward. "What if we could help? I mean, we all see you almost every day, right? What do *we* remember about those days before the accident?"

Liz huffs. "She was hardly talking to me. I'm sure I don't know anything of any use."

Maggie chews on her bottom lip, thoughtful. "What was going on that week? I need a frame of reference for my memory."

Cally taps on her phone and studies the screen.

Liz looks over her shoulder. "That would have been the week of Abby's birthday," she says, referring to our youngest sister. She straightens a little. "We had a party at Mom's."

Maggie nods and her face brightens. "You were there, Hanna. And something happened, because you were upset."

"I remember that," Liz says. "She took Abby aside after we sang 'Happy Birthday,' and when you two returned to the party, you both looked happier. Like you'd settled something."

Next to Monday, Liz writes *Abby's party.*

"What else do we remember?" Maggie says.

The girls look to each other, and after several beats of silence, I sigh. "It's okay. I'll figure it out."

Cally yawns. "I'm so flipping tired. You guys mind if we call it a night?"

Liz raises a brow. "It's seven thirty."

Cally shrugs. "I'm pregnant."

"So," Maggie says, crossing her arms, "am I the only one who wants to know how *that* happened?"

"Yeah," Liz says. "I thought Will couldn't have kids. Weren't you guys looking into adopting?"

Nix frowns. "Does someone want to fill me in?"

Cally's cheeks turn pink. "William had a football injury in high school that made it highly unlikely he'd ever be able to father children."

Nix inclines her chin. "Yes, but medically speaking, *highly unlikely* is not the same as *impossible*."

Liz smirks. "Especially if you're fucking like monkeys."

Cally puts her hand on her stomach and smiles. "As it turns out."

When the girls leave, I stare at the notes Liz left behind. My eyes skim over *Abby's party* and land on all the blank spots. Something filled my time and my head during those days, and something led me to put on Max's ring when I knew that would mean saying goodbye to Nate. *Something*. But what?

I'm climbing into bed when my phone vibrates on my bedside table.

> **Nate:** *Meet me at the park for lunch tomorrow. I promise I won't kiss you unless you ask me to.*

NINE

NATE

The leaves crunch under my feet as I pace in front of the swings, waiting for Hanna to meet me.

I texted her the invitation last night, but she didn't reply until this morning, and when she did, all it said was *1:30.*

My watch says it's twenty-five after, and my empty stomach is yelling at me about the breakfast I was too nervous to eat. Whether Hanna can understand it or not, today is a big day for me.

"Beautiful day, isn't it?"

I spin around at the sound of her voice, and for a moment, I can only stare at her. She's in jeans and a pink T-shirt that says *Coffee, Cakes, & Confections,* and she looks so damn beautiful with the autumn sun shining on her skin that I want to break my second promise this week. I want to kiss her.

My gaze drops to her left hand and her bare ring finger.

"Who told you?" she asks.

"Asher."

He found me out back late last night, after I'd put Collin to bed. He told me that they broke up and warned me to be careful. When I promised I wouldn't hurt her, Asher grunted and said, "Maybe it's not her I'm worried about."

Hanna sighs. "This doesn't change things between us. The babies are my priority right now. I don't need any additional confusion in my life."

And that's pretty much what Maggie told me this morning. I don't know much about fighting for women—it's never been something I've wanted to do. But with Hanna, I know that fighting for her is going to mean equal parts patience and persistence. I'll give her the space she needs.

"I know," I say. "That's not why I asked you here."

"It isn't?"

"Collin," I call to my son. "Come meet my friend."

Collin hops off his swing and runs over to us, his dark mop of hair falling in his face.

"Hi." Hanna looks stunned. "You look so much like your daddy."

"Hi!" Collin replies. "I'm Collin, and you're very pretty."

"I'm Hanna," she says, dropping to her knees. "You're charming like him too."

Collin grins. He loves it when people tell him he's like me in any way, so Hanna's just outdone herself without knowing it.

"When I get big, I'm going to get a Hulk tattoo just like his, but he said I have to wait because it hurts a lot."

Hanna nods. "That's a good plan. Do you like the Hulk like your dad?"

"Of course," he says. "Don't you?"

Hanna smiles and stands. "I guess I don't really know enough about the Hulk to feel one way or another about him."

"We'll teach you." Collin looks up at me. "Won't we, Daddy?"

Swallowing the lump in my throat, I nod. "If she wants us to."

"She wants us to," Collin says. "Don't you?"

"Sure."

"Hanna's the friend I was telling you about, Collin. She's very special to me. Do you know why?"

Collin studies Hanna for a minute then looks up at me. "Because she knows Spider-Man?"

Hanna bites back a grin. "I'm sorry. I don't know Spider-Man or any of the superheroes, actually."

"Hmm," Collin says thoughtfully. "Then it must just be because you're so pretty."

I have to bite back a grin of my own. She's going to think I told him what to say. The truth is, my kid just has really good taste.

"Hanna's pregnant," I finally say. This is going to affect Collin's life, and I have no intention of keeping it from him. "She and Daddy made babies, and those babies will be your little siblings."

"Really?" Collin asks, staring at Hanna's belly.

Hanna looks up at me, caution all over her face. "It's true. They'll be twins, like your dad and your aunt Janelle."

Collin's eyes go big. "I'll have a brother and a sister?"

"I don't know," she says. "Maybe. Or maybe two brothers or two sisters."

"Will you live with us in our house?" Collin asks.

Another look from Hanna, this one less cautious and more apprehensive.

I jump in. "No, buddy. Hanna lives here in New Hope, and we live in Los Angeles."

"Then we'll have to visit a *lot*!" Collin looks at me. "Can I go play some more?"

"Sure," I reply. "Just stay where you can see me."

Collin loves New Hope. He's spent more than his share in the concrete jungle of cities, and he loves walking down to the river or even just going to the park, where the playground is surrounded by trees and filled with kids whose parents have never hired a nanny in their lives.

When he's across the playground, Hanna expels a long breath. "He's precious."

"He's my world." I need her to understand. "Or he has been until now."

She studies me for a minute. "You didn't have to do that."

"Do what?"

"Introduce me to your son. Tell him about my pregnancy."

"He was my everything, Hanna. But the day I met you, my world expanded."

"Nate—"

"Whether you're going to be with me or not, you're going to be part of my life." I close the space between us and press my hand to her stomach. "*They* will be part of my life."

"At least they'll have a big brother who loves them."

I swallow.

"Having three children in two different parts of the country is going to be a lot more complicated than what you're used to."

"My invitation stands. I would love to have you live with us in LA. I would give you anything you need, anything you want."

"Except my life in New Hope," she says softly. "You can't give me that in LA."

"Daddy!" Collin calls from the top of a twisty slide. "Look at me!"

I watch Collin slide down. "When is your next doctor's appointment?"

She drops her gaze to her hands. "Three weeks."

"I'll be there." And maybe by then she'll have had enough space and time from her breakup to reconsider my offer. "In the meantime, promise me you'll let me know what you need. Say the word, Hanna."

HANNA

I've always felt a special bond with my youngest sister. She's twelve years younger than I am, so we're not super close the way I am with Liz, but we understand each other in ways our other sisters can't.

Abby is petite, where I've never been, but we've both had to contend with the efforts of our fat-phobic mother our whole life. In my case, it was because I was actually overweight, but Abby's love of dance gives Mom the excuse to harp about calories. We're both a little screwed up as a result.

I find Abby in the basement doing a Zumba video, which, I must say, is a marked improvement from the running Mom used to make me do. At least Zumba is fun for kids.

"Hi, Hanna!" she says when she sees me. She grabs the remote and clicks off the TV then dries herself off with a towel. "No worries," she says, still out of breath. "That's my only workout for today and I ate breakfast."

"Gotta have fuel," I say softly.

After collapsing onto the couch, she grabs her water bottle from the end table and unscrews the top. "I hope you're here to tell me your *news*."

Well, I wasn't planning on having this talk today, but I suppose she'll want to hear it from me. "Sounds like you already know."

She rolls her eyes. "I heard Mom crying to Carol about it on the phone. Is it true? Nate Crane is the father of your babies, and that's why you and Max aren't going to get married?"

"Nate Crane is the father," I say carefully.

"How did that happen?"

How do you explain to your eleven-year-old sister that you're a dirty ho-bag who was sleeping with one man while pretending to be with another?

"It's complicated," I answer. "Definitely not the way I intended to start a family."

She sighs dreamily and leans her head into the couch cushions. "As if Max wasn't amazing enough, now you have Nate Crane. I mean, come on! How lucky are you?"

"I don't exactly *have* Nate." Guilt twists my gut, but I smile and say, "But I'm not here to talk to you about that."

"Okay, then what?"

"I'm trying to piece together what happened those last few days before my accident, and I'm wondering if you could help."

She frowns. "How?"

"Your birthday party was that week, right? The girls told me I talked to you alone that day, and it seemed like it might have been something important."

The smile falls off her face and she drops her gaze to study her hands in her lap. "Yeah, I guess so."

"Abby, would you tell me what we talked about?"

She shrugged. "I don't want you getting mad at me again."

My stomach squeezes in dread. "Why was I mad at you?"

"Because I was exercising too much and wasn't eating, and you caught me stealing your diet pills," she says in a rush. "But you don't need to worry anymore. I'm being real healthy."

Oh, God. I pull her into my arms and stroke her hair. "Because you saw me doing all that stuff, right?" I whisper.

She nods against my chest and sniffs before pulling away. "But you said being thin wasn't making you any happier and your habits weren't healthy."

I bite my lip, emotion threatening to spill over. "They weren't. Not at all. But I bet you're the reason I went to the psychiatrist to get some help. I bet you're the reason I decided to be better to myself."

She gives a half-smile. "You promised you would. We both promised." She leans into me, and I wrap my arm around her, hugging her again. I'll have to keep an eye on her now that I know, but I believe what she's telling me.

"It's hard living with Mom, isn't it?" I ask. "She isn't the most reasonable mother around."

Abby snorts. "I caught her researching Paleo diets and children. I know she means well but…"

"Yeah, I know what you mean. When I was a teenager, I wanted to change the spelling of my name to H-A-N-N-A-*H* because the missing last *h* felt like she was trying to make me smaller from the moment I was born. Everyone knows Hannah's a palindrome." I chuckle softly at the memory.

"Why didn't you change it?"

"Because it makes me different." I smile. "And I didn't want to disappoint Mom. I make a lot of decisions because I don't want to disappoint someone. I see you doing that too."

Abby shrugs. "We talked about that already."

"We did?"

She nods. "Yeah, and you promised me you'd always be here for me, whether I disappointed you or not," Abby says. "You said you were going to stop traveling so much."

My breath catches. "I did?"

"Yeah. You said you wanted me to be able to come to you when I was feeling depressed about my weight and stuff. Of course, then you had your accident, and I didn't want to remind you that you were ever mad at me."

"Well, I'm not *mad*," I tell her. "Only concerned because I've been through exactly what you're going through now."

She sighs. "Yeah, and look at you now."

I swallow. "Yeah. Look at me now."

TEN

NATE

"Turn around and close your eyes," Hanna instructs.

I lift a brow. "And miss the show?"

She props her hands on her hips and points to the opposite wall of the doctor's office. "Around."

"Killjoy," I mutter, and to make it clear just how much I resent having to look the other way while she strips, I rake my eyes over her before I turn.

Being in the doctor's office with Hanna is bringing back memories of Vivian's pregnancy. Only everything is different this time. When Vivian found out she was pregnant, we weren't really even dating anymore. I was young and terrified, and I had no idea how much a baby was going to change my life—no idea that a child could change the very construction of my heart.

It's different with Hanna, and not just because I'm experienced. It's different because I'm so painfully in love with her that the idea of her and two of my babies all being in that one body nearly paralyzes me with fear. Keeping my distance these last few weeks was harder than I'd anticipated, but I knew she needed the time.

"Okay," she says, and when I turn back to her, she's sitting on the edge of the exam table, covered by an ugly, white-and-beige-checkered gown. Her cheeks are flushed and she's avoiding my gaze. "Thank you for coming today."

"I wouldn't have missed it." The words surprise me by catching in my throat, and she finally lifts her eyes to mine.

Anything Hanna was about to say is lost when the doctor walks into the room. She does a double take when she sees me. "Oh. Hi. Mr. Crane. Wow. Hanna's told me a lot about you. I'm Dr. Reid, but you can call me Nix. I'm a friend and a fan."

I grin as I take her hand. By her blush, you'd think I was looking up her skirt. "It's always nice to meet a fan."

She chews on her bottom lip for a minute, and when I'm convinced she's completely forgotten the reason we're here, she turns to Hanna. "Congratulations on making it to your second trimester. How are you feeling?"

"Pretty good," Hanna says. "The morning sickness has let up and I'm not quite as tired anymore."

"That's great news!" Nix looks at me. "And how's Dad handling the pregnancy? Are you ready for this?"

Hanna's eyes dart to me then Nix. "He's not… I mean, we're not living together or anything, Nix. He's just the dad."

Just the dad sounds way too much like *just the sperm donor,* and I don't like that. "Yet," I mutter. "Not living together *yet*."

Nix's eyes go wide for a moment. Then she begins her exam—poking at Hanna's hipbones and feeling her belly as she asks questions. Hanna hides it well beneath her clothing, but when her belly's exposed, I can see where it's begun to round with pregnancy, and I'm irrationally jealous that Nix gets to touch her.

"Shall we take a listen?" Nix asks. She pulls a giant bottle of jelly from the wall and uses the Doppler to smear it over Hanna's stomach. While she searches for a heartbeat, we listen to the *whoosh-whoosh* of the womb, and I take Hanna's hand.

Our eyes connect as the *whoosh-whoosh* becomes the sound of our baby's heart. *Dear God.* I forgot how amazing that sound is. How inconsequential the rest of the petty bullshit feels when you're listening to the tiny, miraculous heart of an unborn child.

"There's baby one," Nix says. "Sounds great."

Hanna squeezes my hand as Nix rubs the Doppler over a

different location on her belly, and again, all the whooshing is replaced by the beautiful drumbeat of a baby's heart.

"And there's baby two."

HANNA

I wish I knew what he was thinking. His face looks almost pained as Nix turns off the Doppler and wipes off my belly, but I can't read him.

"I did some research," Nix says. "I didn't want to refer you out to just anybody, but I called some colleagues who work in Indianapolis and found an awesome obstetrician for you."

Frowning, I reposition my gown and sit up on the table. "What do you mean, refer me? I want you to be my doctor."

She tugs her bottom lip between her teeth. "I can't do that. Not in good conscience. Even if there weren't other concerns about your pregnancy, the fact that you're pregnant with twins is enough of a reason for you to see a high-risk doctor. Add to that the less-than-ideal health you were in when you got pregnant and I think it would be best for you to be in the hands of a specialist."

I feel the blood drain from my face. "You think there could be something wrong with my babies."

"That's not what I'm saying." She places her hand on top of mine. "I'm just saying I want you to have the best care possible. You have enough to worry about. The quality of your prenatal care shouldn't be on that list. Shall we set up your appointment for you?"

I nod. "Okay."

Nix grins. "Don't look so glum! You're in your second trimester—this is as good as it gets. The morning sickness will go away, and the worst of your breast tenderness along with it. You'll get your energy back. Enjoy it. Do you have any questions for me?" She looks back and forth between Nate and me.

"Not right now," I say.

"You can get dressed, then. I'll see you out front."

I wait until she leaves the room before turning to Nate, and I find him staring at me.

"May I walk you home?" he asks.

"Sure."

Without being asked, he turns around while I get dressed. We make our way up front, bundle into our coats, and step outside.

"I have to leave in a couple of days," Nate says after we've walked a couple of blocks. "Collin misses his mom, and I need to take care of some things in LA."

"Oh." I shake my head, trying to make the disappointment scatter. He sends texts to check on me, but it's not like we've been spending time together over the last few weeks. I guess I just found his nearness a comfort. "How long will you be gone?"

He shoves his hands in his pockets, and his breath puffs out like smoke in the cool air as he exhales. "A couple of weeks at least. I've been away too long, and I need to take care of some things if I'm going to spend time here after the babies are born."

I draw in a breath. "You're going to spend time here?"

We're outside my bakery, but he stops and turns to me, tilts my chin up with his fingers. "When I say I'm going to be in their lives, I don't just mean I want my name on their birth certificates. I mean the dirty diapers and the sleepless nights."

"It's just…not convenient."

"Worthwhile things rarely are." His eyes go hooded, and his hand doesn't leave my face.

"What are you thinking about?"

His gaze drops to my lips. "You."

I swallow. "What about me?"

"How much I want to kiss you."

My heart stumbles. Because I want him to kiss me. And I shouldn't.

"Do you remember my kisses, angel?" He skims his thumb over my lower lip, and something churns in my belly—hot and low and hungry.

"I remember." My mind instantly conjures a catalogue of kisses. Outside the club, the cool air on my face, the brick against my back. In his pool, my naked body pressed against his. On his bed, his dark eyes intense as he slid into me for the first time.

He lowers his mouth until it's just above mine, his breath warm and sweet against my lips.

"Don't."

He groans so low I can hardly hear it. "You want me to."

"You promised you wouldn't until I asked," I remind him.

His mouth moves to my ear, and his lips graze the sensitive shell as he speaks. "You're going to ask, Hanna. We both know you're going to ask."

"We can't be lovers."

"What *can* we be?"

"Friends."

HANNA

"Now you can open your eyes."

I do as my mother says and find myself face to face with...an open field. "Okay..."

"This land is for sale. I thought you could build your house here." She picked me up from the bakery, and we drove for thirty minutes. Out of New Hope and into stretches of cornfields that are conveniently located near more cornfields.

"Where are we?"

"Just a little drive outside of New Hope, but isn't it beautiful?"

"I don't have any money to build a house," I say cautiously.

"Well, sure you will—after you and Max get back together and you get married. You'll have your trust fund. I can just see you building out here, raising the babies in it, having a big yard for them to run in, and you can host dinners and we'll all drive over to see you."

I burst into tears, but it feels more like I'm smacked upside the face with them. "I don't want anyone to have to drive to see me," I snivel. "I don't want to live in LA and I don't want to live in the middle of a bunch of cornfields half an hour from my family. I want to live in New Hope. I want to be there when Abby starts dating and when Maggie has babies. I want to be here to watch Lizzy's preschool turn into the best preschool for miles and when you get old and senile." I draw in a ragged breath. "I don't want to leave. Is there something so wrong with that?"

Mom's face softens. "No. There's nothing wrong with that at all." She draws me into her arms and strokes my hair. "Nothing at all."

"I'm not going to get back together with Max," I say. "I can't marry him. It's over."

"What? Why? Is this about that rocker? Are you going to be with *him*?"

"No. Yes." I shake my head.

It's been weeks since I gave Max his ring back, and he's been as wonderful as he ever was before. He's been helping at the bakery while I've been doing interviews to replace Liz, he's brought me groceries when he thought I might be too tired to shop, and two nights ago, I caught him applying non-skid surface to the stairs to my apartment. He's sweet and wonderful. The terrifying months waiting before me would be so much easier if he were by my side.

"You still love him," she says into my hair. "I don't understand why you're doing this to yourself."

I pull out of her arms and take a deep breath. "I need to ask you a favor, and I want you to consider it before you say no."

"Okay."

"Max is the silent partner for my bakery, and I want to buy him out. He's trying to get custodial rights to his daughter. He needs the money." If he had the money, he might be able to hire more help at the club again, and he needs time more than he needs anything else. Sam and Will have been helping when they can, but that only goes so far. "Could you give me access to my trust so I can buy him out? I'm not asking for any more than that. Just enough to buy out his portion and pay off the mortgage on the building."

She studies me for a minute then shakes her head. "I would if I could, but those trusts were established by your father. We'd have quite a court battle on our hands if we wanted to go outside his terms, and we'd probably lose." She sighs. "I know this is important to you, and I'm sorry I can't change that."

My eyes burn with tears. Stupid hormones. "It's okay. I'll figure out another way."

ELEVEN

HANNA

The night is gorgeous. The stars twinkle on the river and the moon bathes Asher's backyard in a soft glow. Maggie and Asher have been in New York together the last week, and they've invited us all here for an early Thanksgiving gathering.

Nate's been gone for nearly four weeks, and I keep finding myself wandering around the party, looking for his face. I know he's coming back to town soon because he said he'd be back in time for my ultrasound next week, but every time I scan the faces in the crowd, I come up empty.

"We want to thank you all for coming," Asher announces to his guests. "We're thrilled that you could come on such short notice. You see, this isn't just any party. We wanted you to celebrate with us."

"Go ahead," Mom calls. She's practically bouncing in her seat. "Tell them your news."

Asher and Maggie exchange looks, and Liz says, "Holy shit. You're pregnant too?"

Maggie laughs. "No. That's not it. But"—she sticks out her left hand toward the small crowd—"we're married."

"No way," Liz breathes, and then, suddenly, everyone is

clapping and cheering, and Liz and I are rushing toward Maggie to hug her.

When I get my turn, I squeeze her tight. "Congratulations. You deserve this."

Maggie returns my hug. "I'm so happy. I never thought I'd get to be this happy."

"We want details," Liz demands.

Maggie beams. "We were in New York visiting Zoe, and Asher took me to this gorgeous little vineyard upstate. He had everything arranged—the flowers, the location, the photographer. He said he knew I was afraid of weddings because of…well, you know…but he didn't need a big crowd. He just needed me. If I would have him."

Tears spill from my eyes because I can picture everything she described, and as much as I would have loved to be there, I also know that Asher gave Maggie exactly what she needed.

"What did you say?" Liz asks.

Maggie looks at Asher. "I said, 'I do.'"

Before long, music is playing, drinks are flowing, mounds of food cover the buffet tables at the back of the house, and Liz and I have found our spots near the dance floor in the basement where she has access to the bar and I can more easily do my pathetic crowd-scanning thing without being obvious.

"Hey, Liz," Sam says, running his eyes over her in her black dress. "That dress looks terrible on you. Want me to help you out of it?"

"You wish," she grumbles.

He grins and dips his head to her ear to whisper something I can't hear. Whatever it was makes her smile despite herself, but she shoves him softly and says, "Go hang out with your boys. I'm talking to my sister."

When he's gone, I raise an eyebrow at Liz. "So, are you going to tell me what's going on there?"

She crosses her arms and frowns. "Nothing. It's *Sam.*"

I sigh. "Well, if you aren't going to use what he's offering, can I borrow it?"

"No," she snaps. Her eyes track Sam across the room.

Holy crap. I think Liz has a thing for *Sam.* And not just an "I'd fuck him" thing. An *emotional* thing. Where have I been?

Some emotion I don't recognize flicks over her face before she pastes on a smile that would probably fool anyone but me. "I mean, I think you could do better, but go for it."

Not a chance. Not when my twin is giving him the hot-and-needy eyes. I don't need Sam anyway. Just sex.

I sigh. "I'll find someone else. Why did no one ever tell me how horny being pregnant makes you? Because this is ridiculous."

"Seriously?" Liz snorts. "You've got two sexy guys who'd kill to climb into bed with you and you're going to complain to *me* about being horny?"

I wave away her objection. "Too complicated. I just want sex. A lot of it. As often as possible."

"You called?" a deep voice says behind us.

I turn and find myself staring into Nate Crane's intense, brown eyes. Holy cow, he's sexy, and the way he drags his eyes over my body makes me want to strip off his clothes, crawl on top of him, and take exactly what he's offering. What was I saying about complicated?

Nate nods toward the dance floor and offers me his hand. "You owe me a dance, angel."

Mute with longing, I follow him and let him pull me into his arms. He's warm and his chest is solid against my cheek. He smells so good it makes the muscles between my legs clench.

"God, I missed you," he murmurs in my ear.

My stomach flip-flops. "You shouldn't say that."

"What? I can't miss my *friend*? Are you going to tell me you didn't miss me at all?"

Only every other second and the ones in between. "A little, I guess."

"How are you feeling?" he asks against my ear. Then I can feel his lips curve into a smile as he adds, "Other than painfully horny, that is."

My cheeks burn. "You weren't supposed to hear that."

"Maybe I'm glad I did. Maybe I wanted an excuse to talk my way into your bed."

I bite my lower lip. Hard. Because I would gladly take him up on that—even if I know I shouldn't. And it's not just because pregnancy has left me as horny as a teenage boy at prom. It's because it's Nate, and I know a little bit about what would happen if I let him talk his way into my bed. But I'd like to know more.

"We can't," I protest lamely, because apparently my brain has conquered my girly bits in the battle for control of my speech. "You know that."

NATE

When I walked into the party tonight, she was the first thing I saw. In a black dress and bright red heels, she'd catch any man's eye. With her belly rounding with my babies, I could hardly see anything else.

I brush a lock of hair behind her ear. "All I know is that we're two consenting adults who want and love each other. All I know is that you're having my babies, and I'm going to be part of your life from here on out, whether you want me or not." It's one thing if she doesn't want to be with me, but I'll be fucking damned before I let her fantasize about screwing some other man just to get off. "Come with me," I say, taking her hand in mine. "I need to show you something."

She narrows her eyes. "What?"

I don't answer, but she doesn't argue as I lead her away from the party and up two flights of stairs from the basement to Asher's second floor.

"Nate," she says, the warning apparent in her voice as I lead her into my bedroom.

"The balcony," I say, pushing the doors open.

The night is balmy and the cool air nips at my cheeks, but I needed to get her away from everyone else. I needed to get her alone.

Her shoulders relax a bit as she walks to the rail and settles against it. "It's beautiful tonight," she murmurs.

There she stands. Gorgeous and framed by moonlight that shimmers on the water and stars that spread out across the black sky.

"Stunning," I whisper. Coming up behind her, I place my hands on the railing on either side of her. "And so are you." She stiffens slightly, and I graze the side of her neck with my lips—not kissing exactly, but definitely pushing the limits of her "friendship" rules. Damn, she smells good. Like vanilla and lavender. But I want her to smell like sex and me.

She's so fucking beautiful in that dress—a black thing that shows off her curves and ties above her rounding belly. It's grown in the weeks that I've been gone, and since I walked into the party half an hour ago, all I could think about was getting her alone and tugging on that bow, getting my hands on what waits beneath.

"What are you doing, Nate?" she asks, but even as she says it, she's tilting her head to the side and giving me better access to her neck. *Hell yes.*

"I'm trying to help a friend," I whisper against her ear, my hand finding the tie in the front of her dress. "You said we're friends, right?"

She stiffens slightly.

"Don't overthink this, Hanna. Just relax." I tug on the tie, and she gasps. The dress loosens and opens.

"We shouldn't," she says as my hand closes over her breast.

"Are you asking me to stop?" I pinch her nipple, and she moans, arches into me. I release her breast and trail my hand down her body, circling her navel.

"Didn't you say you weren't going to do this unless I asked?"

"I said I wouldn't *kiss* you unless you asked. I didn't say anything about putting my hands on your body."

"You don't play fair."

"Fuck fair. For you, angel, I'll play downright dirty."

She places her hand over mine and guides it farther south until my fingertips are brushing the satin band at the top of her panties. It's all the permission I need.

Sliding my hand into her panties, I find her wet and swollen. "Is this what you need?"

I roll her clit between two fingers, and she gasps. "Please."

"I'm the only man for this job. Do you understand?" I release her clit and cup her softly.

"Nate, please."

"Please *what*, angel? Tell me."

"Touch me," she whimpers.

"I don't want anyone else touching this body," I growl, sounding and feeling more possessive than I ever have in my life. The idea of her fucking Max, the idea of him inside her, his hands on her body—it's enough to make me crazy. "No one but me."

"I don't want anyone at all," she objects, but her body betrays her and she rocks into my hand, begging for more.

"But I think you do." I run a finger along her clit, my touch light, more a tease than a gift. "I think you want me very much." Then I slide my fingers inside her, and she's so wet and so tight that my cock aches.

She lets her head fall to the side. I kiss her neck and play with her breasts as I fuck her with my fingers, making her mine in this simple way.

"Tell me you don't think about me when you're alone in your bed," I whisper. "Tell me you don't imagine my cock inside you when you're getting yourself off."

With a soft moan, she rocks her ass back, grinding against my hard-on.

"I'll tell you what I think about. I think about my face between your legs. Your clit under my tongue." Taking her earlobe between my teeth, I suck hard, showing her exactly what I'd like to be doing to her clit, and she comes, her pussy pulsing tight and hard against my fingers.

She turns in my arms, and the movement pulls my hand from her panties. Her teeth are sinking into her bottom lip and her eyes are still dark with lust. "Thanks, I think."

I raise a brow. "You *think*?"

She bites back a smile. "I don't want to encourage you."

"I don't need any encouragement to get you off, angel." I slide my hands down her back to cup her ass. "Just permission. Let me take you home. Let me…" I stop the words before they can leave my tongue. *Let me make love to you.* "Let me fuck you, Hanna."

She draws in a ragged breath. "I need to get back downstairs before…"

I wait for her to finish. *Before someone realizes we're both gone.* The words hang between us unsaid.

MAX

Will can't take his eyes off Cally. Asher can't take his eyes off Maggie. And, in a new and unexpected development, Sam can't take his eyes off Liz.

I need to get away from all the sexual tension in this party, so I wander the house. I haven't seen Hanna since I arrived late. I was hoping for a dance or, hell, just a smile. I'd take it.

She's been so tired lately with the pregnancy and putting in too many hours at the bakery. I wouldn't be surprised if she went home early. But when I pass the guest room on Asher's second floor, I hear her voice out on the balcony.

I smile as I follow it and then freeze when I spot her. She's standing at the railing, but Nate is behind her, his body pressed against hers, his mouth at her neck…and his hand between her legs.

Jealousy blazes through me at the sight. It doesn't matter that she's not wearing my ring anymore. The moan that slips from her lips feels like a betrayal, and I have to turn and leave the room before I yank him off her and throw him off the fucking balcony.

HANNA

"You don't need to go anywhere but my bed." Nate's breathing is hard and his eyes are hot. He leans down and brushes his lips against my ear. "Tell me you don't need me inside you."

I shiver, and when he offers his hand, I take it.

He leads me into his room. After swinging the door shut and locking it, he slips my untied dress off my shoulders. "Lie down," he commands, his voice rough.

I glance at my red heels.

"Don't touch them," he commands. "Last time I had you keep your heels on, I didn't get to fuck you. This time, I'm going to."

I know I should object. This isn't smart when we both know this will only complicate our future relationship, but I can't muster the will. When he removes his clothes and settles onto the mattress next to me, I can't bring myself to feel anything but gratitude.

"Have I ever told you how beautiful you are?" he murmurs. His hand sweeps over my collarbone, between my breasts, and over my belly, and when it dips lower, I part my legs instinctively, needing his touch there.

"You're beautiful too." And it's beyond true, but maybe the more amazing thing is the "too" on the end of my statement. Because I've never doubted Nate's attraction to me. It's been there from the beginning—from that first moment our eyes met in the bar. When he's looking at me, I am beautiful, and maybe that shouldn't matter, but after a lifetime of feeling unattractive, he was exactly what I needed. Maybe what I still need.

His fingertips are following invisible paths up and down my thighs, his eyes locked with mine. I arch my hips off the bed, telling him with my body where I need his touch. He just smiles.

"Don't rush me, angel."

I trail my fingers down his solid chest and follow that soft trail of dark hair south of his navel until I find what I'm looking for. "You sure?" I ask, wrapping my fingers around his thick shaft. A thrill flutters through me at the raw need that comes over his face as I stroke him. "Now," I whisper. "Please. I need you."

He groans and finally—thank you, God— settles his hand between my legs. He moves his fingers over my clit, teasing me before sliding a finger inside me.

My breath leaves me in a rush because, *damn,* I needed this. I needed what he did on the balcony, and I need this, and I need more. His hand rocks over me, his palm applying just enough friction against my clit as his finger pumps in and out. I keep my hand wrapped around his dick. I stroke and squeeze, desperate to bring him the same pleasure he's bringing me.

His teeth nip my ear. "I wanted to do this all night," he whispers, his fingers still working their magic between my legs. "I heard what you said to Liz, and I wanted to kill Sam and then take you to a dark corner and fuck you so hard your legs wouldn't hold you up."

I gasp as he shifts the angle of his hand, and I can hardly *think*, let alone explain that what I said about borrowing Sam was a joke.

He moves so quickly—drawing up my knees and positioning himself—that he's inside me before I realize what's coming. The quick and unexpected stretch and pressure of him filling me throws me over the edge. I cry out, squeezing and pulsing around him as I fly over that amazing edge of pleasure, and my body spasms.

When I recover and open my eyes again, he's resting on one elbow and stroking my cheek. His eyes are dark and hungry, and he slowly resumes his movements and thrusts into me, pressing deeper with each thrust.

"Again, angel." He hooks one arm under my knee and draws my leg up higher, and when he fills me, it feels so good I scream.

I rock against him as he murmurs dirty encouragements into my ear, his words urging me along.

"Your body was made for mine," he whispers against my ear. "Just enjoy this." Then he thrusts hard and deep and we come together, my orgasm squeezing him as he comes inside me.

Only after does he break his promise. He takes my face in his hands, gentle and sweet, and he kisses me like I'm the only thing in the world that matters.

"I didn't ask you to," I object when he pulls back.

His lips curl in a self-satisfied smirk. "I'm not even a little bit sorry."

TWELVE

HANNA

"I want to know exactly what happened between you and Nate at Asher and Maggie's party," Cally says to me, wriggling her brows.

"I think he fucked you silly," Liz adds, "and you don't even have the courtesy to let us live vicariously."

The Wire is crowded tonight, and despite the ruckus around us, I still feel like everyone can hear our conversation.

"Can we please talk about something other than my love life for a minute?" I plead.

Liz sticks out her lip like a pouting child. "Your love life is the most interesting thing happening around here at the moment."

Cally raises a brow. "I'm not sure that's true. I heard you're sleeping with Sam Bradshaw."

"What?" Nix crosses her arms and glares at Liz. "I thought we were sisters in sex deprivation?"

"No offense, Nix," Liz says, "but that's not a club I'm that interested in being a part of."

Maggie snorts. "Preach."

"I want details," Cally says.

I bite back my grin and toy with my straw. "Details would be good. Come on, Liz. Have the courtesy of letting us live vicariously."

"I was horny. I slept with Sam. The. End."

"Lame," Nix mutters. "Vicarious sex is all I've got right now, and you're totally failing me."

Liz drains her chocolate martini and stays silent. *Stubborn.*

"I could use some vicarious sex too," I admit. Because my stolen moments with Nate were gone too quickly and only left me wanting more. "Is it normal to be this horny while pregnant?" I ask Nix.

"Biologically speaking?" she asks.

"Totally," I say.

"It's normal to be that horny when a guy like Nate Crane is looking at you like that."

I follow Nix's eyes to the other side of the bar, where Nate and Asher are sitting in a booth, and Nate's eyes are glued to me. The girls look too, and Cally and Maggie fan their hands in front of their faces.

"Tell me again why you aren't fucking him silly," Liz says. "Because there are desperate, undersexed women at this table who are offended by that sexual tension going to waste."

My cheeks burn as I study my virgin daiquiri, but Nix saves me by moving the conversation away from me and Nate again. "You," she says, pointing an accusing finger at Liz, "don't get to call yourself undersexed if you've recently fucked Sam Bradshaw."

"I'm sure he'd fuck you too if you asked," she mutters. She waves to the waitress and holds up her empty glass, signaling for another drink.

Cally snorts. "I'm not so sure he's interested in anyone but you, Liz."

"We're not surprised that you did it," I say, nudging my twin under the table. "More that you waited so long."

"It wasn't the first time," Liz grumbles, avoiding our eyes as the waitress hurries with her fresh martini.

"You had sex with Sam before and you didn't tell me?" I squeak. "What else are you keeping from me?"

"Is he as good as the rumors suggest?" Maggie asks.

Liz scowls. "Why do you think I went back despite my better

judgment?"

"Details," Nix demands.

Liz takes a sip of her martini and licks her lips slowly. I can't tell if she's remembering or trying to figure out how to change the subject. Then Maggie gets struck with the same revelation I had at her party.

"You *like* him," she whispers. "This isn't just sex. You really like him."

Liz shakes her head. "I'm a grown woman, and I'm done playing games. I want something *real.* Wicked-hot sex and handcuffs and the best orgasms ever aren't really a foundation for a successful relationship."

Across from me, Nix actually whimpers. "I really hate you."

"Doesn't sound so bad to me," I say.

Liz shrugs. "I shared. On to someone else, please." She looks to Maggie. "How about you? Can you share some dirty newly married sex stories for Nix to live vicariously through?"

"Do you really think I'm the kind of girl who would kiss and tell?" Maggie asks.

"Yes," we all say in unison.

She snickers and turns in the booth to eye her husband across the room. When she turns back to us, she has that wicked smile on her face. "He's still got it." She turns to Cally. "And married sex is the best, wouldn't you agree?"

"Yes." Cally grins. "But married, pregnant sex is even better."

I sigh. "Lucky bitches."

"Where are we?" I rub my eyes, trying to wake up.

After he promised he wouldn't try to get in my pants again, I let Nate drive to my doctor's appointment in Indianapolis. We had lunch afterward, and I must have fallen asleep on the way home. Now, we're parked on the street in front of a house I don't recognize, and the sun is sinking lower in the sky. We're in the newer part of New Hope, in the recently developed area by the river where my mom and Asher live.

"Are we visiting someone?"

Nate doesn't answer me. Instead, he climbs out of the car and walks around to open my door. When I step onto the sidewalk, I see a "For Sale" sign in the front yard and a "SOLD" magnet across the center of it.

I turn to him and narrow my eyes. "What is this?"

He shifts awkwardly and gives me a tentative smile. He actually looks *nervous.*

"What are we doing here?" I ask again.

The house is beautiful. Not as big as my mom's and definitely not the size of Asher's, but it's a Cape Cod-style home with a covered wraparound porch and blue shutters.

I follow Nate to the door, and he produces a key from his pocket to unlock it. "Why do you have a key?"

"I know the owner," he says, pushing through the front door.

Whoever sold the house must not have moved their furniture out yet, because right inside the door is a fully furnished living room—fluffy, overstuffed couches, oversized chairs, all situated around a soft beige rug.

I'm still not sure what we're doing here, but I follow Nate into the kitchen. He turns on lights as I take in the dark cabinets, gleaming countertops, and shining appliances. The sink sits under a big picture window that looks out into a large, fenced backyard.

"Could you live somewhere like this?" Nate asks quietly. "It's not right on the river like your mom's and Asher's places, but I thought this might be safer for the twins. You can let them run out back and play without having to worry about them going too close to the water."

"Sure," I say. "Someday, this would be great." But this is a house for a family—a couple of kids and their parents. Not a screw-up single mom who loves two men and doesn't deserve either of them. Someone with a steady job who can pay the mortgage, not a floundering new business. "For now, I'm fine in the apartment above the bakery."

Nate shoves his hands into his pockets and his shoulders draw up around his ears. "No, you're not."

"That's hardly your choice to make."

He raises a brow. "You think I shouldn't have a choice in where my children live?"

"That's not what I meant."

"No? I think it was. I think you're still convinced that, by the time you have those babies, I'm going to be back in LA and out of your life for good." He stalks up to me slowly, determination in his eyes. "Sorry to disappoint you, angel, but that's not going to happen. You can't push me out of your life."

"I'm not trying to!" I squeeze my eyes shut and take a breath. We had such a nice, pleasant day, and I don't want to ruin it. "I never want to make you feel like you aren't welcome in the twins' lives. You're their father. They'll need you." I lift my gaze to his, and he drops his shoulders.

"So let me do this," he says softly. "If not for you, then for them."

"Do what?"

"Give them a home. This home. I know you think you can make it work in that little apartment, but even if it weren't way too small for two children, it also has those damn stairs. Have you really thought about what it's going to be like, lugging two babies up those stairs along with strollers and groceries? And what about when it gets icy in the winter? What if you fell again? What if you were holding the babies when you fell?"

I let out a long, slow breath. He's right. That apartment isn't going to work once the twins are here. "Okay," I agree. "I need a different place to live, but I'm not in a position to have a place like this yet."

"I am."

I wrap my arms around myself and shake my head. "No. It's too much. I can't let you do that for me."

"I already have," he says softly.

He takes my hand and leads me through the house—the breakfast nook beside the kitchen with a great view of the backyard, the dining room.

"The master is on the main floor," he says, "but there's an attached office you can use as a nursery until the twins are old enough to move upstairs." He takes me into the large bedroom.

The attached bathroom is gorgeous—stone countertops, a jetted tub, and a large tile shower that has room for a small family. Off to the left of the bedroom is a sunny room with dark mahogany nursery furniture—two cribs, mechanical swings, a rocking chair, and a changing table.

"Do the current owners have twins too?" I ask.

"I'm the current owner," Nate says. He watches me carefully. "I bought the house and furniture for you. I hope you like it. I didn't get any of the bedding or decorations because I thought you'd want to choose that."

My breath feels stuck in my throat and my eyes burn with unshed tears. "It's too much."

He gathers me against his chest and wraps his arms around me. I'm so overwhelmed that I let him, breathing in his good, clean scent and wishing life were simpler.

Suddenly I'm hit with a memory of Vivian crying in my office, asking me to give her a future with Nate. He deserves that future. And if it weren't for me, he'd want it.

"It's not nearly enough," he whispers against my hair. "You're carrying my children. There is no gift that amounts to that."

"Thank you."

"I tried to remember everything you told me you wanted in your life. It's close to your family, so someday, when Maggie has kids, the cousins can play. It's a five-minute drive from the bakery. The fenced backyard will be perfect for a dog when you decide you're ready for that."

I pull out of his arms and wipe my eyes. "You thought of everything."

"I tried." He studies me. "There are four bedrooms upstairs, so the twins can each have their own room when they're older, but there's still room for more kids if that's what you want."

I chuckle softly. "And who exactly would I have these children with?" I regret the question as soon as it's out of my mouth.

Some emotion I don't recognize flashes over Nate's face, and then he's stepping toward me, cupping my jaw in his big hand, skimming his thumb over my lips. "May I, angel?"

I'm too caught up and trying to process his nearness—the

amazing and forbidden unfurling of need low in my belly—and before I realize what he's asking, his mouth is on mine. Warm and tender, coaxing and wicked, the kiss is everything that turns me on about this man. It's the sweet against the sensual, the protective against the need to consume. His lips sweep over mine and his tongue slides into my mouth, and I feel wanton and sexy and cherished all at once. I want to stay here, locked under the power of his kiss as his hand slides under my shirt. I could. I know he'd take me as far I as I wanted to go, and it would feel so damn good.

Between my shirt and bra, his thumb grazes over my sensitive nipple, and I gasp at the faint contact. My knees go weak and the hot, needy ache between my legs turns molten.

Somewhere deep within me, I find the will to step away from his kiss, and we stare at each other, chests heaving, eyes hot, bodies on fire.

"You bought me a house," I say. "You didn't buy me." But my mind is already conjuring up all the things we could do in that bathroom, and some really horny, slutty part of me is whispering that it wouldn't be right to let him buy me that big four-poster bed without trying it out.

Some of the heat has dissipated from his eyes and his jaw is hard. "I'm not some asshole who's trying to buy you off. I didn't kiss you because I think you owe me."

"Then why did you do it?" I ask.

"Because you were looking at me like you wished I would."

I swallow the guilt gathering in my throat. "It's too complicated. We're going to be in each other's lives. We need to set boundaries."

"You still want Max."

For a minute, I can only blink at him and wonder how he thinks Max has anything to do with this. I'll accept this gift because it's done and I know he can afford it, that he'd insist if I argued. In reality, I'd rather have him—here, in New Hope, making *me* his first family. I'll accept the house because I can't ask for more.

"I don't want anyone."

He flinches, and for a moment, I wonder how I learned to lie so quickly.

HANNA

Three Days Before Hanna's Accident

The bell at the front of the bakery dings, and I head up front to find a leggy, raven-haired beauty, her lips parted slightly as she studies my shop. A tall, blond Viking of a man follows behind her, his broad shoulders filling up the doorway. There are more dead-sexy men in this city every day.

"May I help you?" I ask, tearing my eyes off her young-Fabio companion.

"This town is unreal," she says. "Like something out of a movie. So flipping cute."

I can't help but grin because most people dismiss New Hope as a dumb, little hick town. I appreciate anyone who can see it the way I do. "Thank you. I think so too. Would you like some coffee? Breakfast? The scones are especially delicious, I'm told."

"Oh, I'd love a cup of green tea if you have it." She flushes sweetly. As she looks at me straight on for the first time, it hits me—this isn't just any out-of-towner. This is Vivian Payne. The actress. The mother of Nate's child. "Does asking for green tea make me sound like Los Angel-bitch? Little bit, right?"

"Not at all." I fill a cup with hot water with remarkably steady hands and grab a tea bag before handing them to her across the pastry case. "On the house. What brings you to New Hope?"

"I'm hoping to track down Hanna Thompson?"

That's what I was afraid of. I force a smile. "You're looking at her."

"Oh! Wow. Crap. Well, no wonder."

I arch a brow. There is no way I can dislike this woman. Sweetness and goodness roll off her in waves. Why couldn't she just be a bitch?

"No wonder what?"

"No wonder Nathaniel's in love with you," she says softly.

Nope. Definitely not a bitch. "Thank you…I think." I can't risk having anyone overhear this conversation. I've worked too hard in the last few months to make sure everyone in this town thinks that Max and I are still together, and now that I know what Max has done for me… "Do you think we could talk somewhere private?"

Her eyes light up. "I would so appreciate that!"

I call to the back for Drew, and she scowls at me as she takes her place in the front. Her aversion to working with the public isn't as bad as she likes to let on, but she still likes to make a big deal about it every time I ask her to work the front.

Her scowl falls away when she spots Fabio. "Can I get you anything?" she asks, teenage lust dripping off her words.

"Drake," Vivian says, and I'm honestly disappointed his name isn't Fabio. "Get yourself something. I'll be back up shortly."

While leading Vivian to the back of the kitchen, I do my best to act casual, as if having her here isn't completely intimidating to me. "Have a seat," I say when we get into my office.

"This place is just adorable," Vivian says. Maybe from any other Hollywood starlet, that would sound condescending, but it doesn't come across that way from Vivian. She sips her tea and looks around my office with what appears to be sincere interest. "Why would you want to leave this behind?"

I frown. "What?"

She blushes. "I don't mean to presume, but I thought you'd be moving into Nate's house?"

My stomach pitches. "Did he tell you that?"

She bows her head. "Listen, he'd be really upset if he knew I was here. I had to harass Jamaal just to find out anything about you. But I'm sure you understand that I have good reason to be worried."

"Worried about what, exactly?"

"Nate doesn't fall in love easily. I just want to make sure that you're after him for the right reasons."

I shift in my chair and attempt to lower my hackles, but it doesn't matter how sweet this woman is. The assumptions behind this conversation are insulting.

She raises a hand. "I know how that sounds, and I apologize."

"What makes you think I'm *after* Nate at all? Maybe he's the one *after* me." Yeah, my attempts to calm myself? Big, fat fail. But *damn*.

Vivian's eyes fill with tears. "Must be nice."

Well, crap. "Do you want to tell me what this is really about?" I ask, calmer now.

"My husband and I divorced."

"I'm sorry to hear that."

She shakes her head. "No, don't be. It's what everyone expects of an actress anyway, isn't it?" She sighs. "I want my son to be raised seeing what love can be. How intense and beautiful, and how deep it can run. I didn't have that with my ex-husband. Maybe I could have, but you can't love someone the way they deserve when half your heart still belongs to someone else."

"And you love Nate."

"I never stopped," she whispers. When she lifts her gaze to meet mine, her lashes are damp. I swear I've never seen anyone look so pretty from crying. "But loving someone means wanting what's best for him, and if that's you, I won't confuse the issue. But if that's not you..." She studies me for a moment. "If that's not you, I'd really like you to step aside so my little family can have a chance." Her voice pitches at the end, and a tear escapes and rolls down her cheek. "We *are* a family, you know. Despite everything. I just want to be sure you know that."

I think of Nate's face when he talks about Collin. How desperately he wants to be the best father possible to his son, how he'll do anything to be part of Collin's life. "It was nice to meet you, Vivian." I stand and open the door to the office, motioning her out.

We walk up to the front together, and Max and my mom are at the front, chatting with Drew. Max's face lights up when he sees me. He skims his eyes over me in a way that reminds me too well of what used to be between us.

"Hey, beautiful," he says softly, pressing a kiss to the corner of my mouth.

Vivian's eyes shift between us, confusion on her face. "You'll think about what I said?" she asks. She doesn't wait for an answer before pushing out the door and leaving.

"You can't love someone the way they deserve when half your heart still belongs to someone else."

I'm already thinking about it.

I thought this would be an impossible choice, but there's only one choice that will give both of the men I love the lives they want.

I grab Max's hand and drag him to the back and into my office.

"Are you okay?" he asks, grinning.

I push the door shut behind him and shove him against it as I press my mouth to his, searching for answers in the kiss of a man who used to be my whole world.

He doesn't hesitate but slants his mouth over mine. His hands seek out my curves immediately, one settling on my ass, the other under my shirt just beneath my breast.

He rubs his tongue over mine, and I want to crawl into all his heat and goodness and warmth. I want this to work. I need it to.

He kisses the corner of my mouth and down the side of my neck, and a little moan escapes my lips. His grip on me loosens as he looks at me. "Marry me," he says softly. If I thought he was releasing me, I was wrong, because the hand under my shirt skims the underside of my breast before finding the front clasp of my bra and unhooking it. "And not just because you want me as much as I want you." Hand against my bare breast, he cups me and rolls my nipple in his fingers.

I whimper, but I make no move to escape his touch.

"Not just because I'm dying to get inside you and make you come."

"Max," I warn. My knees are unsteady, but when I wobble, he pulls me closer to him, still torturing my breast and making the whirl of desperate, achy, needy pleasure spiral tighter between my legs.

"The sex is going to be amazing," he whispers, his mouth brushing my ear. "Waking up with you in my arms is going to be a dream."

Effortlessly, he spins me and lifts me onto my desk, sending paperwork scattering across the floor as he steps between my legs. My skirt bunches at my hips, and he slides his hand up my inner thigh.

I grab his wrist and our eyes lock in that moment before my decision. I can stop him or I can let him touch me.

I lead his hand farther north. He groans as his hand connects with the damp lace of my panties. My sweet, tender Max vanishes. He tugs them to the side and sinks his fingers inside me.

I cry out, and the sound echoes in the small office. He sucks my earlobe between his teeth as his fingers pump in and out of me. If he stopped now, I'd die. I need this—and him. My heart hurts, and I need to know that this man can fill the hole Nate Crane will leave behind.

"God, I missed the way you feel wrapped around my fingers," he groans in my ear. "So. Fucking. Sexy."

His thumb finds my clit, and I slide my hips forward, giving him a better angle while pushing my body closer to his.

With his free hand, he yanks my shirt over my head and tosses it to the side. Then he dips his head and sucks my nipple between his teeth—as hard and relentless as the hand fucking me between my legs.

Back arched, hips bucking, hands in his hair, I come. My world shatters into a brilliant blast of light, but as it slowly pieces back together again, nothing feels like it fits.

Max runs slow, soft kisses up my neck and back to my ear. "We're good together, Hanna. And our life together, here in New Hope? I'll do everything in my power to make it all you ever wanted."

I draw in a breath—thick and shaky and ragged.

Suddenly he's holding me in his arms, murmuring, "Don't cry," and kissing away my tears.

I am a collection of mismatched puzzle pieces, and all I want is to feel whole.

THIRTEEN

MAX

"Max! I have great news."

I frown at my phone. Other than when she called to tell me that Hanna had decided to go ahead with the bakery with me as her anonymous investor, I don't think my lawyer has ever left me a voicemail message with good news.

"A lawyer from California has contacted me, and her client is offering to buy you out of the bakery. The numbers she's throwing out are almost too good to be true. They'll more than cover the mortgage and your initial investment and leave you with a nice nest egg for your investment. As we prepare to move forward with your custody case, this would put you in a great position. I think you should take the offer. Give me a call."

I squeeze my eyes shut. An offer on the bakery. Probably from Nate Crane—this would cut me out of Hanna's life, and I'm sure that's what he wants.

My lawyer's right. I need the money. But the bakery is my last connection to Hanna's life, and selling it makes the end of our relationship feel too final. And who is the client? I'm not turning over half ownership of Hanna's *life* to just anyone. If it's Nate, would he use his ownership as leverage to get Hanna to move to LA?

I dial my lawyer, but she doesn't answer. She left the message on my office phone last night—a habit we formed when my involvement in the bakery was still a secret—and I doubt she's in her office this weekend.

After locking up my office, I find Sam at the front of the club. He's covering the front for me this morning—something he's done most Saturdays since I bought the bakery and didn't have the money for staff.

"I need to run over to the bakery," I tell him. "Are you okay to open if I don't get back in time?"

Smirking, Sam nods. Saturday mornings aren't a hopping time for fitness. "Whatever happened to your plans to offer classes on Saturday mornings to get traffic in here?"

I shrug. "I've just had other priorities."

"Like paying the bills for the bakery instead of hiring someone who could bring you new business here."

"Shut up."

"I'm just making an observation. Grab me a cup of the good stuff while you're over there."

"Should I assume Liz knows how you like it?"

"Fuck off," he mutters, but there's a hint of a smile behind the command.

The bakery smells amazing this morning—always, really, but there's an extra hit of vanilla in the air this morning, and it reminds me so much of Hanna's smell that it makes my chest ache.

"Oh, hey!" Hanna pushes through the swinging door from the kitchen and gives me a tentative smile. For a moment, I forget all the bullshit and almost expect her to come around the counter and rise onto her toes to kiss me.

I wish she'd forget too—just for a moment—that those days are behind us. I'd hold her fast and keep her close. I'd deepen the kiss until she softened and moaned against my mouth. I'd remind her what's worth fighting for.

"Thanks for helping me out while I did interviews last week," she says.

"It's not a problem."

"Yes, it is. You have your own business to run, and I know it's hard for you to get away. But I appreciate it. Can I get you some coffee and breakfast as a thank-you?"

"I'll take a coffee. Thanks." She pours me a cup, and we both do our best to pretend this isn't as awkward as hell when she passes it across the counter. "How's the hunt for new employees going?"

"It's frustrating. I've found a couple of part-timers, which is great, but I really need a manager who can take care of the front of the house while I do the baking, and I need a second baker to take over for a few weeks when the babies are born. Drew is good, but she can't put in the hours I'll need."

Nate Crane pushes out of the kitchen, and the sight of him hits me like a punch in the gut. She said she wasn't leaving me for him, and he hasn't been around, so I was starting to believe it was true. Until I found them on the balcony at Asher's last weekend.

"Hey," he says, locking his gaze with mine.

I lift my chin as we appraise each other. He looks at Hanna, and I want to pull her into my arms and hold her tight, to keep her close until he leaves. But I don't have that right, and Nate's not going anywhere. I can tell by the way he looks at her—all that unveiled love and longing. I know the face of a man who would slay dragons for Hanna Thompson, because I see it every time I look in the mirror.

"Do you have any more boxes stashed in the back?" Nate asks.

Hanna shifts awkwardly and shoots me a look. "No, but Liz is bringing some any minute now." She points behind her and edges toward the door. "I have cookies that need my attention."

Then she's gone, leaving Nate and me staring at each other. He opens his mouth like he's about to tell me something, but then he shakes his head and goes back to the kitchen.

I need to follow Hanna and find out what she knows about the offer. Hell, I should have saved myself the trouble and asked Nate. Buying me out would be nothing for him.

But I'm a fucking coward and I'm afraid to go through that door. Will he be kissing her? Touching her? Hanna's probably baking cookies—nothing more—but what I saw at Maggie and Asher's has tormented me for days. A repeat performance might destroy me.

"Hello?"

I turn to the door and find a customer. The petite brunette looks familiar, but I can't place her. Did we go to high school together? Or maybe college? High school's a better bet. Over half of my graduating class left New Hope for college and never came back.

She frowns at me and rises onto her tiptoes to peek over my shoulder. "I'm looking for Hanna. Will she be back soon? I could just wait."

I lift a brow. "I'm sorry, do I know you?" Forgetting people always makes me feel like an ass.

"Oops! I'm Elle." She smiles, and again I feel that sense of recognition, but I just can't place her. "Janelle Crane. Nate Crane's sister."

"Oh." Nate's sister. And a famous actress—thus the recognition. "Nice to meet you."

The bell over the door rings as Sam and Liz come in, their arms full of collapsed boxes.

"I stole Sam so he could help me with these," Liz says from behind him. "I promise I'll get him back in time to open the club."

Sam stops in his tracks two steps in the door, and Liz runs right into his back. "Ho. Lee. Shit," Sam manages.

"Walk much?" Liz says, skirting around him. "Geez." She turns to Janelle. "Have you been helped?"

"Yeah. This guy here is helping me. I'm so rude." She shakes her head and gives me an apologetic smile. "What was your name?"

I fold my arms and watch her as I say, "Max Hallowell."

Her brows shoot up and her jaw unhinges. Suddenly she looks just like her character from *Roommates*. "Oooh," she whispers. "Holy crap. And you're here. Are you…? Did Hanna…? Oh, shit. Wow. Well, who can blame her for ditching my dorky-ass brother? You are a fucking *fox*. Look at those shoulders. Damn. How much can you bench-press?"

I don't answer or correct her. I'm not sure what she knows or when she last talked to Hanna. Sam's still gawking, and Lizzy is scowling.

"Who are *you*?" Liz asks Janelle.

"Elle," she says, offering Liz her hand. "Nate's sister, Hanna's friend. You're Lizzy, aren't you? I've heard so much about you."

Lizzy's eyes go wide and she stares at the woman's hand. "*Janelle Crane*," she says, putting it together. "Janelle Crane knows who I am."

"Janelle fucking Crane," Sam mutters. "Holy hell. You're even more gorgeous in person, which, for the record, I wouldn't have thought was possible. Damn."

Lizzy elbows Sam in the side—hard, judging from the way he doubles over—then drops the boxes and takes Elle's hand. "Have you talked to Hanna since the accident?"

Elle shakes her head. "No, but Nate told me briefly about it when he came to see me in India. Does she remember me?"

"I don't know. Probably. She has most of her memory back."

Sam gathers Lizzy's boxes with hers and stacks them in the corner. "What are all these for, anyway?"

"Hanna's moving," Liz says. Then she shoots me a look and winces—no doubt my surprise is all over my face. "And she probably wanted to be the one to tell you."

"Where's she moving?" I ask. "Someplace without stairs, I hope."

"No kidding," Liz mutters. "There are stairs, but she won't need to use them. I'll let her fill you in on the details."

"Is she in the back?" Janelle asks. "I have to talk to her." Without waiting for an answer or, you know, permission, she pushes through the swinging kitchen door.

Liz and I exchange a worried look before I follow Janelle.

The sounds of squealing women greet my ears as I come through the door. Nate's nowhere to be seen, and the women are hugging like old friends. I'm reminded of those months of Hanna's life that I missed. While we were only pretending to be a couple, she was forming new friendships, falling in love with another man…and getting pregnant.

"I am so glad to see you," Janelle says. "And you remember me, so obviously the *important* parts of your memory are back."

Hanna shrugs. "Most of it, but there are still missing pieces."

"Do you know what caused the accident?"

Hanna shakes her head. "Nix said I probably never will remember that day, unfortunately. What are you doing here? How long are you staying?"

"I had to come see the bakery I've heard so much about—and see my idiot brother—but I came here first. Did the lawyers contact you with the news yet?"

"What news?"

"I'm going to buy out your silent partner. Well, assuming he takes my offer, but it was way generous, so I'm sure he will."

Hanna's eyes connect with mine over Janelle's shoulder. The offer didn't come from Nate. It came from Nate's sister, a sister who thinks Hanna dumped Nate for me.

"Actually," Hanna says, "Max is the silent partner." She nods toward me, and Janelle spins around, her eyes wide.

"Oh. My. God. How romantic is that? Did you know that when you decided to marry him? And I owe you an apology! You know when I called and asked you to go check on Nate, I had no idea about the accident and that you had freaking *amnesia.* Nate was more interested in tequila than filling me in on the pertinent details, but he told me when he came to the retreat in India." She shakes her head. "And I'm sorry I had to ask you to do that. Considering the decisions you'd just made, you were probably a terrible person to ask, but I couldn't think of anyone else he'd listen to."

Hanna smiles, but it's forced. "Do you know about my decisions, then?"

"Nothing was official, but you were pretty determined about your choice."

Hanna's eyes flick to mine and then back to Janelle. "My choice to marry Max?"

"Of course. Where's your ring, anyway? Did you set a date yet?" She flashes me a grin over her shoulder then lowers her voice. "He's so gorgeous, I can't even. And is that why you're moving? Are you going to live together?"

"She's going to live with me."

The girls turn toward Nate's voice at the back door, but I don't turn. Any kernel of hope Janelle's rambling gave me is crushed. Hanna's moving in with Nate.

HANNA

Max looks to me, Janelle, and finally to Nate. Then he turns on his heel and heads out the door to the front of the bakery. I hear the front bell ring as he exits to the street.

Crap. That's not how I wanted that to go.

I don't know how long Nate's been there, but judging from the look on his face, I'd say it's fair to say he heard his twin going on about my choice to marry Max.

I hate the idea of hurting either of them, and I'm killing them both.

"I'm not moving in with you." I stalk toward Nate and prop my hands on my hips. "That was never part of the deal."

Nate raises a brow. "You really think I'm going to buy a house in this town and then bunk with the newlyweds when I visit?"

"What's going on?" Janelle asks behind me. "Hanna, I thought you were marrying Max."

Nate snaps his mouth shut at those words and his jaw ticks.

"I called it off," I whisper. "Excuse me. I need to go tell Liz to stop packing my stuff."

I leave, but I don't go to the front, where I can hear Liz talking to Sam. I climb the stairs to my apartment, shut the door behind me, and sink to the floor.

"She's moving in with me."

If only he meant that as it sounded. If only he meant we could be together, a family who lives in the same house in the same town. But he's committed to another family, and I'm plagued by these questions about a decision I can't remember making.

FOURTEEN

NATE

"See everything you miss when you hole up for months without access to the outside world?" I attempt a smile but it falls flat.

Janelle, on the other hand, is having no trouble smiling. In fact, she's grinning like a madwoman. "It worked!"

"What are you talking about?"

"When I sent her to pull you from your drunken pity party, I was hoping she'd…you know, come to her senses and decide not to marry Max. Of course, I had no idea about the amnesia at the time, and that must have complicated things. But God, you were being such a whiny loser."

"She chose him," I growl. "I made a promise to respect that decision and I was trying not to break that promise."

"What did you promise, exactly? To be a loser who wouldn't fight for the woman he loves? The only woman in the world who makes him happy?" She attempts a scowl, but it's washed away by a smile she can't seem to resist. "But you two are moving in together now, so it's all good, right?" She frowns. "Or are you? She didn't seem so sure."

I drag a hand through my hair. "I bought her a house. I assumed she knew I planned on staying there while I was in town."

"You bought her a house? And she accepted?" She frowns. "That doesn't sound anything like Hanna."

"She's pregnant." The words pummel my heart because I know that, if it weren't for those babies, Hanna would have never agreed to move into a house I bought.

"Get the fuck out. Seriously? And the baby is yours?"

"Babies," I correct. "Twins. I bought her a house so she'd have someplace safe to raise them since she won't leave New Hope."

"Of course she's not leaving. Who the hell wants to live in LA? You're going to have to move out here. It'll be good for you."

"I'm not leaving Collin. I'll just have to visit here as much as I can."

"You can't make a life with someone by 'visiting' them."

"Then I guess it's lucky that she doesn't want a life with me," I mutter.

"You're so sure about that?"

"Where have you been?" I glare at her. "You were just standing there, telling her all about how she chose Max."

"You're kidding me, right?" She points to the door where Hanna left. "She's pregnant with *your babies.* Stop letting your fear of rejection rule you. You love that girl, and she loves you."

"And she loves Max." *She chose Max.* Part of me never believed it. Part of me wanted another explanation for that ring being on her finger when she woke up.

Janelle grabs my shoulders. "When she chose Max, it had as much to do with trying to give *you* the life you wanted as it did with loving him."

"How do you know that?"

"We're friends," she says. "We talk. Man up and fight for her." Silence pulses between us, and when I meet her eyes, she looks as sad as I feel. As if she just realized she lost a battle she thought she won.

"I can't leave Collin."

"I get that you want to be Dad of the Year. We had the same asshole father, remember? But what's better for your son than seeing his dad with someone who makes him happy? You're going to stand there and tell me you think Collin's better off with the miserable lump you become when Hanna's not in your life? Better off with a dad who gets drunk every time his kid's not around because nothing else about his life is worth staying sober for? Make him see that Dad's worthy of love and happiness, and when he's an adult, he'll believe the same of himself."

I shrug her hands off my shoulders and turn away. Fuck. I need a drink. But seeing as how it's not even nine a.m., I opt for a deep breath instead. "What if I'm *not* worthy?" My voice breaks on the question. I might as well be a pubescent boy—Hanna makes me feel about that vulnerable.

"You really think he might be better for her?" Janelle asks, and I don't answer because if I didn't believe that, I would have fought for her from the first.

NATE

Four Days After *Hanna's Accident*

I'm half lost in Asher's song when I see Hanna coming down the stairs with her sisters. The sight of her catches me off guard and makes me miss a whole verse. She's grinning and beautiful, her legs on display in that sexy-as-fuck jean skirt. Happiness radiates off her as if she doesn't have a care in the world. As if she didn't just break my heart.

Asher narrows his eyes at me, and I tear my gaze away from Hanna and find my place in the music, hide behind lyrics and harmony like I have most of my life.

Asher transitions into "Unbreak Me," and I follow, harmonizing as he sings to his woman. When the song's over, he leaves the stage to kiss the shit out of Maggie, and jealousy rips through me. I've always appreciated what they have, but I've never been jealous of it. I never thought I could have it for myself, so I didn't bother with wanting it. But then there was Hanna.

I start playing her favorite song before I realize what I'm doing, and when I lift my gaze to hers, she's looking at me, and I'll be damned if I don't understand a single emotion on her face. I should have seen this coming. She hasn't answered my calls or texts since our fight in LA. Then, when I got her message saying she hoped we could talk when I got to town, I assumed the best.

But she chose him and didn't even have the courtesy to warn me, and now she's looking at me like my mere existence confuses her.

It hurts too much to look at her. She's everything I want and can't have. She's everything I would turn my world around for, and I fucked it up.

So I refocus on my song and the lyrics she loves so much.

I'm nobody's hero, baby. Try not to fall too deep.
I'm nobody's angel, love, but you were crying in your sleep.
I'm useless, empty, nothing, sugar. Wait around and then you'll see.
You thought you'd find your answers, but now you're lost in me.

I wrote this song for Vivian before Collin was born. She wasn't in love with me. She was in love with the idea of me. And then she got pregnant and was tied to me—a man who was nothing like the man she deserved. Not so unlike Hanna.

My throat grows thick, but I swallow back the emotion and lift my head to watch her as I sing the last verse. I'm almost surprised when she keeps her gaze locked on mine—that same pain and confusion in her eyes that I saw earlier.

I end the song and leave the makeshift stage. I can't do this. I can't pretend I'm not in love with her. I can't pretend she didn't steal my heart and throw it away.

Up the stairs and out the back door, I find myself heading down to the river that runs behind Asher's house. I have to leave, because if I stay, I'll drink, and if I drink, I'll drag her into my bedroom and beg her to reconsider. If I drink, I'll break the only promise I ever had the courage to make to her.

To think I climbed into her bed last night, ready to promise so much more.

"Stop!" The sound of Hanna's voice stalls my feet, and for a moment, I dare to hope she's following me to tell me she's changed her mind. "Who are you?"

I wince and then turn to her. "Is that supposed to be funny? Pretending there was nothing between us wasn't enough? You need to pretend you don't even know who I am?" And *fuck fuck fuck*, this hurts. Did I really let myself believe it could work out differently? That she might choose me? That, for once, I'd be first choice and not the castoff?

"I—I don't know who you are," she says slowly. "But maybe I should? I was injured and I have amnesia, so I honestly don't know you."

What the hell? "Amnesia? You're kidding me." I take a step forward, remembering the bruises I saw at her apartment last night.

"I'm not." She holds up a hand to stop me. "I'd prefer you to stay over there. Please."

"Amnesia." Please God, let this mean she didn't choose him.

"Yeah."

"You don't know who I am."

"I don't know who you are or why you would crawl into my bed in the middle of the night. I don't understand why—" Her eyes fill and tears stream down her cheeks. Tears I'm desperate to kiss away. I just want to hold her, to whisper in her ear until her body relaxes in my arms. "I don't understand," she repeats.

"You don't remember anything?" God, what are the odds? "Do you know who you are?"

"Yeah. I remember everything up until about a year ago, but the last eleven months are just…gone."

Which means every single moment with me is gone. I drag a hand through my hair and exhale slowly as I try to wrap my head around this new information.

"Do I know you?" she asks.

Better than anyone else in the whole world. "Yeah. You do." My chest is tight and my throat thick, but I take a chance and say, "I'm the idiot who's in love with you."

"But I'm engaged."

"I saw that." I look to her hand again, and again, that damn ring is staring back at me. But maybe... "Can I ask? Did that happen before or after the amnesia?"

Her tongue darts out to wet her lips. "Before."

Any hope her amnesia story gave me deflates just like that. "Fuck."

I hold her gaze for a minute, wishing her memories back. I need Hanna, my Hanna, whole, complete, and with her memories—if not for forever, then for the goodbye her injury stole from me.

I'm the one who looks away. "I've gotta get out of here, Han."

"Please, tell me what happened. What did I do?" she whispers. "I don't understand."

I shrug, but I don't look at her again. I can't. It's already too hard to breathe. "What's there to understand? You're wearing his ring."

When I rejoin the party in the basement, Asher narrows his eyes at me then looks at the stairs and back to me. He must have seen Hanna follow me out. I just shrug and head to the bar.

I've been seeing Hanna for three months, and the only people who know about it are Hanna, my sister Janelle, and Jamaal. I was just the rebound guy, and she didn't want anyone to know. I had no idea how much I could regret such a secret. Would she be engaged to Max now if he knew she spent her summer naked in hotel rooms with me?

I turn to the bar and reach for the tequila. I stop because it reminds me of Hanna. Of the first night we met and the day we made love. I snag a beer instead and lean against the wall to drink.

A clean-cut guy in a navy dress shirt sidles up to me. "I'm Sam, a friend of Asher's," he says.

"Nice to meet you, Sam." He offers his hand. I shake it reluctantly. I'm really not in the mood. "Nate Crane."

"See that blonde over there?" Sam says, nodding his head to the side.

Liz, Hanna's twin, stands beside Maggie, sneaking glances at me and giggling. From the way she's looking at me, it's fair to say Hanna never told her about what is—*was*—between us. Never told her twin and best friend in the world. This should tell me something about just how much I meant to her.

"She's got her eye on you," Sam says. "But she's mine. I just want that to be clear."

I raise a brow. "Isn't that hers to decide?"

Sam just grins. "Oh yeah, and she will. Don't worry."

I shrug. "No problem, man." Not that I'd go near her anyway. Maybe some guys like that kind of revenge, and God knows that, if Hanna had her memories, nothing would hurt her more than my sleeping with her twin. But no matter how battered my heart, I'd sooner shoot off a testicle than hurt her like that.

Asher waves me back over to the stage, and I go reluctantly. Better if I don't let on about my broken heart.

"How about this," he says as I sit down.

I take the paper from his hands and study the lyrics. Then I grab the pencil and make some modifications. "I love it. Wanna try—" The words get lost because Hanna's on the stairs again, her eyes locked with mine.

She turns around and jogs back up the stairs as if she can't bear to be this close to me. When I look back to Asher, he's watching me. He saw the way we were looking at each other. He knows me.

Pretending the silent exchange between Hanna and me didn't just happen, I jot down the last line of the chorus and hand the paper to Asher.

He sighs. "Your lyrics suck today."

"Thanks."

His eyes go back to the stairs as if asking if Hanna's the reason, but I play dumb.

I have to get away from this fucking party, from Asher's knowing eyes asking questions I don't have the right to answer. I head upstairs to call Janelle, but my phone isn't in the basket where I left it. Before I can think where it might have gone, I spot Hanna on the patio, my phone in her hands, and I'm instantly moving in her direction. She's staring at the screen, scrolling through something, and I hope to God it's our text messages. I want her to see. I want her to remember.

Her cheeks are flushed and her lips are parted, and when she lifts her head, she pulls in this little gasp. It sounds so much like the noise she makes when I put my mouth between her legs that my fucking cock goes hard.

"See anything good?" I ask.

Her pink cheeks turn crimson. "Why would I risk everything?"

Right. Losing Max is the risk. Fuck. Nothing changes. "You'd have to ask your fiancé."

"You know why I can't do that." Standing, she pushes her chair back and lifts her chin. "I want to understand. I need you to talk to me."

"No, I don't." Because she's made her choice. What would come of rehashing our mistakes?

"You don't understand what this is like. Not remembering? I'm planning a wedding to this man I've wanted most of my life. Don't I owe it to him—don't I owe it to myself—to have the truth out there before we promise until death do us part?"

Planning a wedding. The words are like red-hot ice picks in my chest.

"I just need answers," she says. She steps closer, tempting me without knowing it. "I need the truth," she whispers.

"The truth? Is that what you really want, angel?" Suddenly, I want to give it to her. I want to put my mouth against her ear and describe in outrageous detail all the things I did to her body. I want to slide my hand between her legs and prove she still wants me—even if she can't remember.

I take another step closer, and when she turns away, I close the distance between us, trapping her between the house and my body as I lower my mouth to her ear.

"Do you want to know what it was like between us?" I ask.

"Yes."

I groan. "Should I start with how wet you were every time I touched you? Or maybe how you begged me that first night?"

"I didn't."

"Have you been telling yourself some wicked rocker seduced you? That I tricked you into my bed? Sorry. You asked for the truth. You begged. Right there outside the club, you begged me until I ripped your panties off and you were too busy biting my neck to talk anymore. Is that what you're hoping to remember? How you wanted me so badly you let me finger you out in the open, against that building where anyone could have seen?" I just want her to remember. I need her to remember it all and then look me in the eye and tell me she's choosing him.

She lifts her hands to my chest, but right when I think she's going to push me away, she curls her hands into my shirt, and I groan again because my control is hanging by a thread and threatening to snap.

I can't help myself and I put my mouth to her earlobe, nip at it with my teeth in the way I know makes her crazy. The crack of thunder overhead reminds me of our first night together, the way the sky opened up outside the club and we got soaked. Then, later, when I peeled those wet clothes off her and warmed her with my hands and mouth.

"You might have forgotten me," I whisper now, "but you still like dirty talk, don't you? And maybe if I made you come now, you'd still scream my name. Because you always screamed my name, Hanna. Never his."

She gasps. "You are horrible."

"What are you really upset about? That you wanted me? Or that even as you stand here wearing his ring, you're secretly hoping I'll tell you about it. Secretly wishing you could remember all the details."

"I don't." She shoves me back then, and I'm grateful because I was seconds away from taking her mouth like I'm so desperate to. "Tell me why I did it," she says. "I need to understand."

Looking away, I fight to steady my breathing. What the fuck did I think I was doing? "I made you a promise," I say carefully. I'm reminding myself more than telling her. "I promised that when you made your decision, I would respect it. That if you took his ring, I wouldn't try to change your mind."

A promise I all but broke just now. And as much as I want her—need her—more than she'll ever know, I could never forgive myself if I stole the future she chose.

"I always knew you deserved better than me," I say, still not looking at her. "I hope he's worthy of you. I sure as fuck wasn't."

Only when my breathing is steady and I think I have the strength to touch her without losing my mind do I turn. I take her hands, meaning to retrieve my cell phone, and for three painful beats of my heart, my gaze snags on her lips and I indulge in the fantasy of one last kiss. She'd let me. I can see it in her eyes. She feels something for me, even without her memories. I want to tell myself that means something. If we have a connection without her remembering anything about me, doesn't that have to?

But nothing changes the fact that she chose him.

I take my phone and walk away into the night. When the skies open and rain pours down, I welcome the deluge and wallow in the memories it brings.

I'm sitting in the dark on Asher's front porch soaking fucking wet when Asher finds me.

"I'm sorry I bailed on the rest of the party." I offer him the joint burning in my hand, and he sneers at me.

"You're fucking kidding me, right?" he asks.

"Sorry." I snuff it out and slide the rest of the joint into my pocket. It wasn't doing shit for me anyway. Nothing can erase Hanna from my mind. "Didn't mean to piss off the straight-edger."

"This isn't about the pot and you know it."

I lift my gaze to his. "What's it about, then?"

"What's between you and Hanna?"

"Nothing," I mutter.

"I saw the way you looked at her tonight, and you're a terrible fucking liar."

"Better than an accomplished one, I guess," I say, parroting Hanna's words from the night we met.

"What are you doing?" Asher presses.

"I'm not doing shit. She chose him." I release a humorless chuckle. "And now, conveniently, she can't even remember me."

"Please tell me you haven't been fucking around with Hanna. I told you she has a boyfriend."

Yeah, he told me that the night we met, but it wasn't true. But that's Hanna's secret to share, not mine. "I believe he's now her fiancé."

"He's a good guy, you know," Asher says.

"That's what everyone seems to think."

Asher turns his back to me and looks up at the starless sky. The rain has stopped, but the clouds loom overhead, dark and ominous. "Did you know an anonymous investor set Hanna up with the bakery?"

"Yeah."

"It was Max. That's the kind of guy we're talking about here. The kind of guy who would sell his house and live in a shit apartment to give the woman he loves her dream. The kind of guy who would do it without getting any of the credit or the glory."

"Then how do you know?" I ask.

"I know people." Asher shrugs then turns back to me. "I'm not trying to be an ass, but I care about Hanna, and I want what's best for her."

"And you know that's not me?" That hurts. Especially from Asher.

"Think it through for a minute. You dodge commitment, and Hanna deserves better than that. And even if you were willing to give her more, how's that going to work? Are you going to move to New Hope to be with her and leave Collin in LA?"

Resting my elbows on my knees, I lean forward and study my shoes. Asher's pulling out the logic I've been trying to make myself accept ever since I saw that fucking ring on her finger. Hanna belongs here, in this little picture-book town with its friendly people and quiet streets. And I belong in LA. Near Collin.

"Do you have any idea how much I hate being away from my daughter?" Asher says. "Three months in the summer, two weeks over Christmas and a couple of long weekends here and there—that's all I get until I can convince her mom to give me custody. You know I have reasons beyond Maggie for staying away from the city, but I don't see you making that kind of sacrifice for a woman. Am I wrong?"

"She chose him," I repeat, because—*fuck*—I don't need to hear this. There's nothing to figure out. She doesn't want me. She's wearing his ring.

And I have to find a way to be okay with that, because a big damn part of me knows she chose right.

FIFTEEN

HANNA

My apartment is a clutter of half-packed boxes, and my mind is a jumble of questions and missing memories.

When I walk into my living room, Nate is bare-chested and sitting on the couch with his bare feet propped on the ottoman. For a minute, I forget how to walk. My feet seriously don't recall the order of operations necessary to get me from this spot at the edge of the kitchen island to the family room coffee table, where I left my cell phone.

Because Nate. Because bare-chested. Because hormones eating away at all the functioning parts of my brain and leaving only the parts that want sex.

I don't know if his presence—his *body*—is evidence of a divine power that loves me or one that wants to torture me. My mouth is dry and my hands itch to touch, to trace the lines of his tattoos and the faint trail of dark hair from the center of his chest all the way down past his navel and into his jeans.

I've followed that trail with my mouth before, and sweet, sweet memory, I know what waits on the other side.

When I drag my eyes back up to his face, he's smirking at me. "See anything good?"

"I was going to ask you the same thing. And then I was going to ask you to please refrain from watching porn in my family room."

"Wanna watch with me?" He wriggles his eyebrows and spins his iPad so I can see the screen. Comics. Of course.

"How'd you get in here?" The question comes out with a squeak.

"With the key you gave me last summer. God forbid anyone see us together if I was in town, so you gave me a key so I could come in the middle of the night."

I draw in a ragged breath at the bitterness in his tone. *"God forbid anyone see us together."* I wonder if it occurred to me how selfish I was being. "Did you ever use it?"

"Once," he says softly. He sweeps his eyes over me in my robe and lets them settle on the knot tied across my growing belly. "I got off the plane from London and hired a driver to bring me straight to you." He sighs. "My phone was dead, so I used the driver's, but you didn't answer. When I got here, I let myself in with the key you gave me and climbed into your bed. Unfortunately, you didn't know who I was, and we both know how that ended. Frankly, if you would have given me that knee to the balls before, you probably wouldn't be pregnant now."

I bite back a guilty laugh. "Sorry."

He shakes his head. "No. I'm sorry. I shouldn't have assumed you wanted me there."

My legs seem to be functioning again, so I walk over to the living area and sit on the chair. He's filling in blanks for me, and I'm desperate to see them filled.

"Tell me what else you remember from those days."

Apprehension flashes across his face. "You'd called me in London. You'd left a message saying you wanted to talk. It was the first time I'd heard your voice since you'd left LA after our fight. You'd been ignoring my calls and my messages. The only reason I knew you were okay was because you were still talking to Janelle, and she assured me you weren't dead in a ditch somewhere. She said you were thinking. You were trying to make some hard decisions, and I needed to give you space. At one point, she even suggested that she could fly out here herself and check on you if it would make me feel better. But then you left that message, and I thought maybe…" He shakes his head. "Obviously, I thought wrong."

"I would have had to leave you that message before my accident."

"Yeah. It was Thursday."

I lift my eyes to his. The day of the accident. Was I calling to tell him I was going to marry Max? "Why didn't you call me back?"

He stares at me a long time then blows out a long breath. "I thought it would be best if we had the conversation in person. And then it turned out you were engaged to him and it became a moot point."

He's silent for a minute, and then his serious face transforms to a smile.

When I realize his eyes have settled on the cleavage peeking out the top of my robe, I pinch it closed. "Sorry. I'll go get dressed."

"I wasn't complaining."

"Yeah, well…" I shake my head. "I'm not going to tramp around in my robes if you're going to be spending a lot of time at the house."

"So you'll move? You'll take the house?"

I've spent most of my day thinking about it, and I nod. "I can't deprive my children of that home when their father wants to provide it. It's not reasonable. And when I stepped back and thought about it, it makes sense that you'd want to stay there when you visit. There's plenty of room and there's no reason you can't claim one of the bedrooms as your own. I just wish you'd considered how you phrased it when Max was listening. I'm sure the idea of us *living together* was a slap in the face to him. We're friends and we're parents together, but we're not a couple. I want that to be clear."

"Crystal clear," he murmurs gently, so much the lion to the sheep.

I sigh and continue. "And when I can, I want to pay you back for the house."

"Hanna—"

"Please." I'm quiet for a moment, trying to figure out how to explain it to him. "You are the father of my children, and I will let you provide for them, but I never want to feel like you're my sugar daddy, providing for his woman on the side." I drop my gaze to the floor because I sure as heck can't say the rest while looking at his bare chest. "And that's why we can't sleep together again. You can't move here. I get that. You'll visit as much as you can, and I'm sure you'll be an amazing father near and far. But if we make a habit of sleeping together when you visit, I'll just feel...convenient."

He pushes off the couch and comes to stand in front of me. My eyes are glued to his bare chest, so he tilts my chin up. "Are you sure you want to make that rule?"

I nod and meet his dark, smoky gaze. "I'm sure."

"If that's what it takes to get you to move into the house, I promise I won't sleep with you until you ask me to."

I snort. "I think I remember you making—and breaking—the same promise about kissing me."

A slow smile spreads across his face as he traces the line of my jaw with his thumb. "It's true. I'm pretty terrible about keeping promises that involve staying away from you." He lowers his mouth to my ear, and I shiver. "How about I just say that, when I touch you, I promise to make it inconvenient as hell." His mouth hovers over mine for a moment, and I can't think or breathe. Just when I've prepared myself for his lips, he steps back and grins. "I guess that means sleeping in your bed tonight is out of the question?"

I blink at him. "I— What?"

"Tonight? I'm not staying with Maggie and Asher. Newlyweds don't need me around. Do you want me in your bed or on your couch?" He drops his gaze to my lips. "I'll do *whatever* you want, angel."

"I—" I swallow. Then again. Because I *want* a lot of things. And he knows it. "The couch."

He rakes his gaze over me one last time before turning back to the living room. "Sweet dreams."

MAX

I'm beating the shit out of the punching bag when Will finds me. He doesn't say anything, just holds the bag and lets me go at it until my knuckles ache from hitting and my shoulders burn from swinging.

"Wanna talk about it?" he asks when I finally admit defeat and sink onto the bench.

"He bought her a house. She's moving in with him."

Will exhales slowly and sinks onto the bench beside me. "Well, fuck."

And that about sums it up. It's not so much that Nate bought her a house. God knows that, with his money, he could buy her any damn thing he wanted. It's that she accepted. Her willingness to move in there proves more than she realizes.

"You bought her a bakery," Will says hopefully.

I grunt. "Not for long."

My lawyer emailed with details of Janelle Crane's offer, and not long after, the actress called me herself about it. I already know that, if Hanna wants me to take it, I will. I need to.

HANNA

The shower rains down on me, hot and delicious on my sensitive skin. Having Nate in the apartment with me last night was enough to make me lose my mind. I lay in bed waiting for him to come into my room, climb into bed with me, and whisper something sexy in my ear.

But he didn't. He stayed on the couch all night long, giving me the space I asked for, even as I wished he wouldn't.

Then we had a long day of packing and unpacking, moving and organizing my belongings in the new house. Liz, Sam, Maggie, and Asher helped, and Cally and Drew took care of the bakery. Janelle helped a little, but she had to leave to meet with Max about her offer.

"You've got a really cool thing going here," she said. "I want to be part of it and never want you to feel beholden to some man."

"I don't feel *beholden* to anyone," I said, but in the end, I agreed that she'd be a less complicated choice as a silent partner and promised I'd talk to Max.

Though Nate and I were too busy to talk much during the move, I'd catch him watching me, and then he'd wink and rake his eyes over me in that way of his. My cheeks would burn and every cell in my body would click into overdrive.

My new shower is amazing. I relish the hot spray coming from three directions. I wash my hair and body, shave my legs—a task that's getting more difficult by the day—and then turn off the water. After drying my body, I apply lotion, giving special attention to my growing stomach. I spent most of my life hating my stomach and wishing it were flat, but now my round belly makes me smile. I'm more than okay with it. I feel beautiful with it. Is that because of how much I already love these babies or because of the way Nate looks at me?

After we got everything moved, Nate went across the street to Maggie and Asher's house. He and Asher are still working on songs for their collaboration, but he made me promise I'd call if I needed anything.

I dry off and dress in maternity jeans and a sweater before walking across the street. It's dusk, and my breath freezes as it hits the air. I knock and no one answers, so I let myself in. The house is quiet, and I assume everyone's downstairs. I head in that direction and find a tall, blond man standing in front of the stairs. It takes a minute before I remember how I know him. Fabio...er...Drake. Vivian's bodyguard.

Before I can ask where they are, I hear Vivian's voice floating up the stairs. "Please reconsider. I'll do anything to make this work."

Murmurs. Nate's voice. But I can't make out his words.

Drake crosses his arms over his broad chest and gives me a look that tells me what he thinks of my presence. "I thought you were marrying the other boy." His voice has the low, gravelly rasp of a pack-a-day smoker, and I think it's the first time I've heard him talk.

I frown. "When did I say that?"

He shrugs. "Last time I visited, you were wearing his ring."

"You ever think she got pregnant on purpose?" Vivian asks in the basement.

I gasp, and Drake says, "That's a private conversation."

"Right," I whisper. Then I turn to the door and hurry across the street to my new house.

Less than half an hour later, Nate finds me in the kitchen. I'm sipping a cup of herbal tea and trying to figure out what to do about what I overheard.

He grabs a beer from the freshly stocked fridge, pops the top off with a bottle opener, and joins me at the table. He looks stressed and frazzled.

"Rough night?" I ask softly.

"You could say that." He takes a long pull of his beer. "Collin told his mom that you're pregnant. She isn't handling the news very well."

"Oh." I didn't really expect him to tell me about his conversation with Vivian, but I like that he is. "What did you say?"

"That it wouldn't change my relationship with Collin. That I owe as much to these babies as I do to him." He picks at the label on his beer. "She didn't care, though. It's my fault she's reacting like this. I shouldn't have let her find out like that. I just wasn't sure how to tell her."

We sit in silence for a minute. I'm unsure of what to say. Nate's picking at his beer label, aggravation rolling off him in waves.

I clear my throat and nod to his beer. "You know they say that people who pick at their labels are sexually frustrated."

My attempt to clear the tension falls flat when he lifts his eyes to mine. There is so much longing and heat and desire in them that it nearly bowls me over.

"*They* have no fucking idea." His chair scrapes across the floor as he stands. "Goodnight, Hanna."

NATE

"It's a nice house," Janelle says, scanning the living room. "You seem at home here."

Hanna's out with the girls, and Collin's asleep with his head on my lap, his chest rising and falling with the steady breath of sleep. I brush his hair out of his eyes and study his face. He stayed with his mom in a hotel last night, but he'll spend the next week at Hanna's new house with me. With Hanna. Then I'll take him back to LA, where he'll stay for a few weeks before Janelle brings him out to visit again. And so begins our new life.

"How's Hanna?"

"She's okay. Exhausted from the move." I shift Collin in my arms and stand. "Let's get him to bed." I take him to his bedroom, Janelle walking ahead of me to draw back the covers.

We head back out to the kitchen, and I pull a beer out of the fridge for myself and pour a glass of wine for Elle.

"Max is letting me buy him out," she announces.

I raise a brow. "You didn't have to do that."

She snorts. "Are you kidding? That woman works magic in the kitchen. This is the best investment I've made in years."

"I have to agree. She's amazing. So, are you planning to move here to be her business partner?"

"Me? In Middle of Nowhere, Indiana?" She shrugs. "God, sounds nice, doesn't it? But no. I'm a silent partner. I don't imagine I'll be around much more than I would have been otherwise."

"Vivian found out about the pregnancy," I say.

She sucks in air through her teeth. "And how'd that go? I'm half surprised she left Collin here with you. I'd expect her to get all Münchausen-by-proxy kind of psycho after that."

"What's that supposed to mean?"

She rolls her eyes. "Seriously? The woman would do anything to keep you to herself."

"I think you're wrong."

She gulps her wine and shakes her head. "And I think *you* are blind."

SIXTEEN

HANNA

Every cell in my body is exhausted. I never would have thought it was possible to be exhausted on the cellular level, but after making Christmas cakes and pastries for every freaking family in New Hope, I have zero energy left and every intention of peeling off my clothes and climbing into bed. When I step into the bathroom to brush my teeth, that gorgeous soaker tub stares back at me, calling my name.

A soak in Asher's hot tub would feel amazing right about now, but since that's off-limits with the pregnancy, a warm bath is as good as it's gonna get for me.

I turn on the water and wash my face and brush my teeth while the tub fills. I strip off my clothes and wrap my hair into a loose knot on the top of my head. I have to grin at the sight of my stomach in the mirror. It's hard to miss. I'm only halfway through my pregnancy, but I already get comments from strangers about how I must be getting close.

As I step into the tub, I actually moan in pleasure at the feel of the warm water on my skin. I turn on the jets and sink into the soft eddies of water.

Without my permission, my mind immediately fixes on Nate

shirtless and beautiful sitting on my couch, Nate winking at me as he helps at the bakery, Nate sleeping in the bedroom over mine. Suddenly I'm not so tired and my skin tingles in the whirling water, so ready for human touch.

NATE

I have developed this nightly habit of tucking Hanna into bed. She goes to bed early, and half the time, I find her under the blankets with a book before eight. Being with her like this—close enough to touch at all times but off-limits—is making me lose my mind, but if my mind's gonna go, I couldn't think of a better way.

I head straight to the master. It's later than usual, so I expect to find her asleep, her book on the pillow beside her. Her bed is empty, but I can hear the jets running in the tub on the other side of the bathroom door.

I knock softly. "Hanna?"

No answer.

I knock again, a little louder this time. "Hanna, are you in there?"

When there's still no answer, my heart kicks into panic mode and I'm picturing her asleep in the tub, sinking into the water and drowning. "Hanna?"

I open the door, expecting to see the worst.

Instead, I find Hanna soaking in the tub, the jets stirring the water around her. But it's her hands that steal my breath—one between her legs and one at her breast, pinching her nipple.

God, she's so fucking beautiful it hurts. Every day that I'm in this town and not touching her causes me literal pain, but seeing her like this—the pleasure on her face as her hips lift and she moves her finger inside herself—is the most delicious kind of torture I could imagine.

Her eyes are closed, and I can't make myself move any direction but forward. I want it to be my hand between her legs, my fingers bringing her that pleasure, and my mouth at her swollen breasts.

Hanna's always been beautiful to me, but round with pregnancy—ripe with *my babies*—she's over-the-top gorgeous.

She shifts her hand between her legs, changing her angle. Her moan is so soft I can barely make it out over the jets.

I'm so fucking hard. My cock strains painfully against my fly. I need to leave. She doesn't want me here. God knows I've made it clear where she can find me if she's interested. But my feet don't obey, and I can't take my eyes from her. What is she thinking about? Who is she imagining touching her?

Max? Me?

She murmurs something. Was that my name on her lips?

I don't dare to hope, yet I hear myself say her name. I speak it softer than I did outside the door, but she hears me this time, and her eyes fly open.

Her lips part and she says my name on an exhale. If I thought she was beautiful before…*damn*. Her eyes are dark with desire, and little tendrils have escaped from her hair tie, curling against the smooth skin of her neck. Her breasts rise and fall with her breath, her nipples teasing the water's surface as she takes me in.

"You're so beautiful."

She surprises me by crooking her finger at me. I step toward the tub as she rolls onto her knees. When I'm near enough that she can reach, she tugs on my belt and pulls me another step forward until she's looking up at me through her lashes and her face is level with the belt she's pulling from my jeans. She unbuttons my pants and tugs them down my hips.

"Jesus," I hiss. But her hand is already sliding between my legs and cupping my balls in her palm as she wraps her other hand around the length of my shaft. "Hanna…"

Her eyes flash to my face briefly before she's positioning her mouth over me—taking me in and stroking me with her lips and tongue—and my hand knots in her hair and tightens because *Christ, that feels good.*

I spread my legs to keep my balance and watch her lips move over me, feel her tongue wrap around the underside of my cock. God, I've wanted this—needed it. Not the blowjob, but Hanna.

Touching me, letting me touch her. When she adds suction, a growl tears from my throat and my hand tightens in her hair. Then she moans too, and the vibration sends a current of pleasure right through me, knotting tight and low in my balls.

The hand that was stroking the base of me falls away. She dips it into the tub and slides it between her legs and—holy fuck—she's stroking herself while she's sucking my dick.

My eyes want to close because it's good. So damn good. And knowing that doing this turns her on that much makes it all the hotter. But I force them open and keep my eyes glued to her—so fucking beautiful. And, for the moment at least, mine.

She pulls me deeper, moaning as she strokes herself, and my control snaps and I thrust my hips—once, twice—as she swallows around my swollen cock and I come.

HANNA

When I pull back and lick my lips, Nate's looking at me like I'm a goddess. Like I'm the most amazing woman he's ever been with or near.

"I wanted to make sure you were okay," he says.

"I'm not," I whisper. "I'm not okay at all."

He cups my face in his hand. "How can I help?"

"Sleep with me tonight," I whisper. I'm sick of being alone. Sick of knowing he's so close and feeling like he's so far out of my reach. "No expectations, no confusion. Just…stay in my bed."

Then his hands are under my arms and he's kissing me and drawing me from the tub. He takes his time drying me off before leading me into the bedroom. I climb into bed, but he doesn't follow. He stands beside it and trails his eyes over me again and again, finally letting them rest on my stomach.

I settle both of my hands on my slightly rounded belly. "Imagine how big I'll be by the end."

He laces his fingers through mine and moves my hands before he lowers his mouth to my navel. "So. Beautiful."

Goose bumps run across my skin under the ceiling fan. He explores me with his mouth—his hot, open, miraculously talented mouth—and trails kisses from my collarbone down my arms. By the time his mouth finds my breasts, my skin is warm and I'm impatient for more.

He cups my breasts in his hands, his lips parted, his nostrils flaring. When he places his open mouth over my nipple, it's with the same tenderness he used on the rest of my body, and it's good—so good—and still I want more. My hands go to his hair and I arch into the sensation. While he draws one nipple into his mouth, he caresses the other, brushing the rough pad of his thumb against the taut peak, and that swirl of warmth in my belly becomes larger, hotter, and more intense as it finds its way between my legs.

"Am I too big?" I ask.

He lifts his head. "Too big for what, angel?"

"I want you to make love to me," I whisper. Then, with a hand to my belly, I laugh. "I'm wondering if I waited too long."

He sighs dramatically and rolls over onto his back. "I guess I'll just have to be on the bottom, but you should know this is terribly *inconvenient.*"

Giggling, I follow him and straddle his hips. "I'm not sure if it's inconvenient or impossible."

He lifts his hips off the bed at the same moment he grabs mine, and in the next moment, he's sliding into me, and I gasp. "Nothing's impossible."

Pleasure knifes through me as I sink onto him, but I force my eyes to stay open. He's grinning, and that smile makes me feel like the most precious thing in the world.

"Inconvenient," he whispers, lifting his hands from my breasts, "but damn if the view isn't spectacular."

NATE

She's curled into me, eyes closed, her hair fanned across my arm, and I want to hold on to her forever. I'm afraid that, if I leave her bed, she'll forget how good we are together, and God knows how long it'll be before I get to touch her again.

"I don't forget to use condoms."

She lifts her head and frowns at me. "I think it will be okay. Unless you're afraid you're going to get me pregnant?"

I chuckle and smooth her hair out of her face. "I'm saying I've never forgotten to use a condom before. Vivian and I didn't, but she was on the pill and I was young and stupid and didn't realize how unreliable the pill is if the person taking it is flighty and forgetful."

"I don't blame you," she whispers. "I forgot too. And now that I have them"—she takes my hand and places it on her belly—"I wouldn't want it any other way." She giggles. "They always get so still when you touch my stomach."

I swallow. I haven't felt them kick yet, though Liz and Maggie have. "I don't forget," I repeat. "And I think some subconscious part of me was very aware of what I was doing the day I took you in the shower. Part of me knew I was risking you being tied to me forever. And that part of me would do anything to make that tie."

Her breath catches and she lifts her eyes to meet mine.

"I'm sorry how I handled everything that day. The truth is, I still don't know what our future together looks like, and that scares me. I'm afraid that, if I don't know exactly what's coming and how we'll handle it, I'll lose everything that matters the most. I panicked, and I almost lost you because of it. And, angel, you're one of those things that matters most to me."

"I panicked too," she admits, "because I was scared I wasn't good enough for you to give everything I wanted."

"I should never have gone to London." I wrap my arms around her and pull her against my chest. "I should have tracked you down here and insisted you talk to me. Insisted we work it out. But I thought I'd already lost you."

"You haven't lost me," she says, yawning against my chest. "I'm right here."

I focus on her breath against my skin, the heat of her body curled into mine. I try to live in this moment, to let the here and now be enough. But as the minutes tick by, contentment remains just beyond my grasp, hiding behind a question I only have the courage to speak into the darkness. "Why did you choose him?"

Her only answer is the steady rise and fall of her chest in sleep.

SEVENTEEN

HANNA

I pad down the hall and up the stairs to his bedroom and find the door cracked. I knock softly before stepping inside. I pick up a shirt from the folded stacks in his closet and press it to my nose, inhaling deeply, taking a hit of his scent. There's a picture of Collin on the dresser, his big grin eating up his face as he points to his Captain America T-shirt.

I'm not sure what I expected to find in here. Pictures of Vivian? A journal confessing that he wishes I'd never gotten pregnant? Some evidence that I've made him feel trapped? I am so terrified of trapping him. But there are no answers here. Only his scent and reminders of what a good father he is that make my heart tug.

What would it be like to let this be real?

I sit on the edge of Nate's bed and bury my nose in his T-shirt. His scent relaxes me so much that I find myself lying down. Just for a minute. Just a little rest before I go to my own bed.

"Angel?"

The whisper pulls me from a dream. Then there's a hand on my face, someone stroking my cheek. My eyes are heavy, but I force them open. I see Nate before I close them again.

"What are you doing in my room?" I mumble.

"You're exhausted," he whispers. "Close your eyes."

I obey because it's too hard to wake up and sleep feels so good. As I drift off to sleep, I feel arms wrap around me, warm breath against my neck.

NATE

I wake to the feel of Hanna's soft curves in my arms, her firm, round belly under my hand.

She slides her hand into my boxers and traces the length of my cock, strokes the tip with her thumb. "I want to touch you," she murmurs. Then she cups my balls, causing me to draw in a breath with a hiss. "I want to put my mouth on you."

My sweet girl and her dirty mouth. I'm a goner.

She takes my hands and positions them above my head, wrapping my fingers around the slats of the headboard. I don't object. I would do anything to keep her in this bed with me, and if that means keeping my hands off her a little longer while she straddles my hips—well, I might die from wanting to touch her, but it wouldn't be the worst way to go. The tie on her robe has come loose, and from this angle, I can see the creamy skin of her breasts. She doesn't stay there long. Stealing my view, she scoots down my body and shucks off my boxers.

"Hanna," I growl. I miss the view and the heat of her against my cock. I release the headboard with one hand and reach for her.

She looks up at me from between my legs, her cheeks flushed, her hair wild around her face. "Behave," she clucks, nodding to the headboard.

"You're wicked." Then I decide I've never been any good at following her rules. Grabbing her, I pull her up my body and roll until I'm on top of her.

She grins. "I might be wicked, but you're naughty."

"Damn straight." I kiss her as my hands work to untie the knot on her robe. I kiss my way south until I've found her breasts. When I suck one pebbled nipple into my mouth, she moans.

"Maybe this isn't so bad," she murmurs. "Sometimes."

Lifting my head, I take her face in my hands and shake my head. "No," I growl, and her smile falls away. "I want more than sometimes and I want more than to be friends and parents together. I want you. Completely and always."

"What if we can't figure it out?" she whispers.

"We will," I promise, sliding my hand between her legs. She opens her thighs and lifts her hips off the bed. "We will."

HANNA

Three Days Before Hanna's Accident

I wait until Max leaves for work before I let myself into his apartment and lock the door behind me.

I head straight to his bedroom and the desk in the corner. Max is neat, and there are only a couple of stacks of papers on the desk—a meal and exercise plan for a client and some information about a new piece of equipment he has in the club.

I turn to the filing cabinet and start thumbing through files, not sure what I'm looking for. He wouldn't exactly label it "Secret File About Hanna's Bakery." But I find a file labeled *Smith, Peterson, and Frank* and pull it.

There's a copy of the agreement I signed when I agreed to start the bakery with the anonymous investor and some other paperwork from the lawyer, but instead of a deed to the bakery, I find papers from New Hope Bank and Trust.

My stomach twists painfully. It's bad enough to know that he sold his grandmother's house to get me the bakery, but knowing that he had to take out additional loans makes me sick to my stomach. No wonder he's been letting employees go in favor of putting in long hours at the gym himself. He's busy paying on the loan he took out for me.

For some reason, my gaze catches on a letter stacked neatly on the corner of the desk. It's addressed to Max, but the name of a local investor jumps out at me. I unfold it carefully, and my stomach sinks.

> *This letter contains the details of the offer we discussed over lunch. I think this deal could be beneficial for us both, and I look forward to speaking with you further.*

"No," I whisper. He can't sell his club. He can't sacrifice his dream for mine.

My phone buzzes, and I pull it from my pocket to see a text from Nate.

> **Nate:** *Heading to London. I miss you already. Been thinking a lot about our conversation. Call me?*

I bring my hand to my mouth to stop the sob that threatens to escape. When I was a little girl, I imagined that one day I'd fall in love with an amazing man and he'd love me in return. I believed love was enough to overcome anything. But love isn't like that. The heart has the capacity to love beyond anything my little-girl self could have dreamed up. And where I once thought love was a journey and the destination was being together, I now know that love is more like a state of awareness, and sometimes its best expression is in releasing the person from your life.

I read the text a second and third time and then delete it before I can torture myself with another read. The text disappears, but the history of our texts stays on the screen.

In one hand, my texts from Nate. In my other, the evidence of what Max has sacrificed for me to have my dream.

I hold my breath as I hit the commands on my phone to delete the entire thread. Then I delete my entire call history, and just like that, my phone's memory of my relationship with Nate is gone.

HANNA

Present Day

"Hey, Hanna." Sam stands to greet me at the bank and shifts uncomfortably as I stare him down. "Is this about Liz?" He's really adorable in that clean-cut playboy-banker kind of way. His light brown hair is clipped short, and his strong jaw is shaved clean. Broad shoulders fill out his suit and tie.

"Not about Liz," I say, and he relaxes visibly.

New Hope Bank and Trust is where Max does all his banking—unsurprisingly, since one of his best friends will inherit the whole thing someday.

Sam motions to his desk, and I shake my head. He works out in the open, and I'd rather keep our conversation between us.

"Somewhere private?"

He nods and leads me into a little office where they talk to clients about loans and such.

"Why didn't you tell me?" I ask the moment he closes the door.

He cocks his head. "Tell you what?"

"When Max got the loan for the bakery, why didn't you tell me he was doing that?"

His smile is so fake that it wouldn't fool a blind person. "I don't know what you're talking about."

"Cut the shit, Sam. Why'd you let him do it? He sold his grandmother's house for a down payment, didn't he? Do you realize what kind of a position that's put him in financially?"

His jaw tightens. "Max is a grown fucking man, Hanna. He makes his own decisions. He didn't exactly consult me before throwing the whole damn world at your feet."

"And you don't approve?" The question comes out too snippy. The fact is, if I'd been in Sam's position, I wouldn't have approved of Max's decisions to fund my bakery.

He shakes his head. "I didn't say that."

"He's in debt up to his eyeballs, and I came to you, didn't I? I see it in my planner. Before the accident, I came here and talked to you about what I'd found in his apartment. He was thinking of letting someone buy the club."

Avoiding my eyes, he nods. "You wanted to know how much he owed on your bakery."

"How much?"

"I wasn't at liberty to tell you then, and I'm not at liberty to tell you now. But I promised you I wouldn't let him sell the club. Will and I had offered to be partners before. I made sure he knew our offers stood."

"Is that all I wanted to know?"

He studies me for a minute before finally admitting, "You wanted to know if you had enough in your trust fund to buy out your silent partner."

Bile rises in my throat. "And what was the answer?"

"More than enough."

"That's why I decided to marry him," I whisper, though I've suspected it for a while now. Ever since I remembered finding that letter in his kitchen. "I was counting on a decision I made for all the wrong reasons and you didn't even warn me."

"I didn't know for sure, and you *were* in love with him." He rubs the back of his neck. When I don't reply, he says, "Max misses you, you know. He's just waiting around like some love-sick puppy, and if you decided you still wanted him, he'd be yours."

"I can't," I whisper.

"He would take good care of you. He loves you so much."

"I know that." My throat grows thick and I swallow back tears. "Is there anything else from before my accident that you think I might want to know?"

"Meredith," he says. "The day you fell, I was jogging on the trail behind the bakery and I saw you two arguing."

All eyes are on me when I walk through Meredith's salon and back to her office, but I don't care. For the first time, I'm taking

Nix's concerns about my "fall" seriously.

Meredith's sitting at her desk, but her head snaps up at the sound of the door closing. "What are you doing here?" she asks.

If I expected her to act like the snotty Meredith who's tormented me most of her life, I was wrong. Instead of sharp, her voice is distant, resigned. Maybe months of rejection are starting to get to her after all.

"I want you to give Max custody of Claire."

She raises a brow. "The choices I make for my daughter's life aren't your business."

"If you don't, I'll tell everyone that you were at my apartment the day of my accident."

Meredith's face goes white. "I thought you couldn't remember that day."

"I don't have to remember to know what happened."

She drops her pen. "How's that even possible? No one else was there."

"Sam saw you there. He saw you push me against the wall and yell at me. Why would you do it? I know you hate me, but I never would have thought you'd try to physically hurt me."

She sits back in her chair. "Clearly you underestimate how serious I am about Max."

I gasp. Because even though I'm here, I didn't really believe Meredith was guilty. "So you pushed me down the stairs?"

She pushes out of her chair. "I didn't do any such thing. I came to your apartment and fucking *begged* you to get out of the way so I could have Max back. And, sure, I punched you in that chubby face of yours, but you had on his ring and..." She clenches her hands. She's sneering now, her hatred and disgust toward me evident on her face. "Whatever. You gave as good as you got. You gave me a fucking black eye, and then you ended up in the hospital and I had to leave town so no one would think I tried to kill you. And after all that, you didn't even want him." Her face crumples and she points to the door. "Get out of here. I'm sorry your fat ass couldn't navigate a simple set of stairs, but I won't listen to you blaming me for that."

"I can't believe I used to be jealous of you." I shake my head slowly. "Now I just feel sorry for you."

"Why? Because I'm a single mom? At least I'm not some whore who got knocked up with a rocker's babies."

"I feel sorry for you because you're ugly, Meredith."

She snorts. "Look who's talking."

"Oh, no. You're plenty beautiful on the outside. Anyone can see that." I put my hand on the knob and pull the door open. "But inside, you're as ugly as they come. That's why Max doesn't want you."

Her face blossoms red. "Get out."

EIGHTEEN

MAX

Brady's is crowded tonight. Everyone who's here visiting family for the holidays fills the bars to escape them.

I scan the crowd, but before I spot Will, Liz grabs my forearm and drags me to the dance floor.

I raise a brow as she wraps her arms behind my neck. "No offense, but my years of crushing on you came to an end when I fell in love with your sister."

She snorts. "This isn't about you, Max. Get over yourself."

I follow her eyes to the other side of the bar, where Sam is watching us with an uncharacteristic amount of jealousy on his face. "I see." Not that I'm terribly surprised. Sam's had a thing for Liz for quite a while. "So what's happening between you two?"

"Nothing." She closes another inch between us and leans her head on my shoulder. "He's not what I'm looking for."

I lock eyes with Sam and raise a brow in silent question. The fact that he shrugs and walks away is more telling than he knows. Sam's never been shy about staking his claim, but the way he feels about Liz has evolved over the last few months.

"Can you imagine what would have happened if it weren't for Hanna?" she asks. "Would those casual dates have turned into something more?" She removes her arms from around my neck and shudders softly as we leave the dance floor. "No offense. It's just that, these days, you feel more like a brother than a potential screw."

That makes me grin. "Damn. If you'd told me two years ago that you saw me as a 'potential screw,' it's fair to say things would have been *much* different between us."

She groans, and Cally hands her a drink. "And then I'd be the one dealing with Meredith's bullshit."

"Yeah," Cally says, "and maybe *you'd* be the one with amnesia."

I frown. "What do you mean, she'd be the one with amnesia?"

"Oh, who knows," Cally says, "but there will always be part of me that suspects Meredith was the one who pushed Hanna down the stairs."

Liz shifts uncomfortably. "I don't think Max needs to hear your crazy conspiracy theories."

"The one who pushed her down the stairs? Are you saying the accident wasn't an accident? Are you saying someone pushed her?"

Cally's face goes blank. Then she mutters a curse under her breath. "I thought he knew."

"Knew what?" The women just stare at me, so my voice holds warning when I say, "One of you, tell me."

"We don't know anything for sure," Cally says. "None of us was there except Hanna, and Nix says Hanna will probably never remember that day, but the nature and extent of her injuries indicated foul play."

"Like someone pushing her down the stairs." *Jesus.* Why did Hanna never tell me this?

"And maybe like someone knocking her around a little before they pushed her."

Liz winces. I feel like the wind's been knocked out of me. Because I know who was at Hanna's house the night of the accident.

When Meredith climbs my front steps, I'm waiting at the front door, my arms folded across my chest. The days are short and the streetlights are already on even though it's barely seven. They throw just enough light on her face for me to see the confusion on her face.

"Where's Claire?" she asks.

"She's sleeping." I don't budge from my spot.

"Well, move over. I want to get her."

"I don't think I want her going home with you."

Her eyes flash with anger. "You can't keep my daughter from me."

"I'm pretty sure the police would have my back on this if they knew what you did to Hanna."

"I seriously doubt the police care about some stupid drama. I don't even think I care about it anymore."

"Assault doesn't fall into the same category as 'stupid drama.'"

"What the fuck are you talking about?"

"Hanna's accident. Her fall down the stairs? You went to her house that night. I know because you came to the gym afterward and mentioned you'd been there. Then you left town for two weeks. I'm guessing with a guilty conscience."

"The only thing I feel guilty about was not acting on my suspicions that she was cheating on you. I could see it in her eyes, in the way she was always mentally somewhere else when she was next to you. I only felt guilty that I'd screwed up too much for you to take me seriously when I told you about my suspicions."

"She never cheated on me."

"Just because she was keeping you in limbo about the engagement doesn't mean it wasn't cheating."

"We were broken up," I growl. She stumbles back and grabs the porch rail, so I soften my voice when I say, "No one knew, but we were broken up."

She blinks at me. "You deserve better than that."

I wave away her objection, trying to get us back to the point at hand. "You're telling me you went to confront Hanna and the same night she happened to fall down the stairs and get bruised up like someone was beating on her?"

"I'm telling you I'd never do anything like that, and you're a fucking asshole for thinking I would." She rolls her shoulders back and lifts her chin. "Now move aside. I want my daughter."

She pushes past me and into the house, and I let her. What else can I do? Claire is her daughter, and I have no evidence that my accusation is true. I can't quite wrap my mind around the idea of Meredith using her fists when she prefers words, dirty looks, and carefully crafted manipulations.

When I enter the house, she's buckling Claire into the car seat.

"You all deserve each other. You deserve Hanna and she deserves her cheater asshole baby daddy."

"What's that supposed to mean?"

"It means everyone knows he's still screwing Vivian Payne. Everyone but Hanna. Hell, if she just looked at the magazines from the week she was in the hospital, she'd know what he was doing in London. But, hey, maybe none of you care about something as silly as *fidelity*."

"Meredith," I begin, but she avoids my eyes and pushes past me as she takes our daughter to her car. "Please stop," I call.

She ignores me, climbing into the driver's seat and pulling away without a word.

NATE

The Day of Hanna's Accident

Hanna's curves slide under my soapy hands. Every sweet moan that passes her lips feels like my reward for the shitty parts of my life.

I step back to get a better look at her and the shower water changes to rain and we're outside the club in St. Louis again, but she's nude and there are cameras everywhere.

She mouths my name but no sound passes her lips. Those deep, dark eyes stare into my soul.

"I'm scared," I say, my voice hoarse.

She nods sympathetically and shifts her gaze to someone standing behind me. Two women appear, and she's in a wedding dress, crying tears I never meant to make her shed.

My phone rings and drags me from the convoluted dream. I force my eyes open and reach for it, but my hand connects with flesh instead of phone.

My head is pounding like a son of a bitch, but I force my eyes open.

The woman moans and curls into me.

Fuck, fuck, fuck.

I haven't slept with a woman since I met Hanna. She walks away from me, avoids my calls for five days, and I'm waking up with some strange woman?

I spring out of bed and drag a hand over my face. My head doesn't appreciate the sudden movement, and I have to catch my balance against the wall as I search my mind for answers.

The phone goes silent, thank Christ. I scan my mind for any remnants of memories from last night. I remember the concert. Then after, I found a pub and some tequila.

I was so fucking lonely.

I called Hanna and got her voicemail.

Stumbling across the room, I find my phone peeking out from under the nightstand on the opposite side of the bed. Seeing the notification light flash at me, I hit the button for my voicemail.

"Nate, this is Hanna." She sounds exhausted. The clock tells me it's noon here, which means it's seven a.m. in Indiana. "I'm sorry I missed your call last night. You must have been out late." Out and lonely as hell, thinking I'd lost her, wondering if I was being irrational. "Are you still coming to New Hope when you get back to the States? We need to talk, but I don't want to do it on the phone. Okay. Just…call me when you can."

I feel like I'm sixteen again, because all I want to do is listen to her message on repeat. Revel in the sound of her voice and dissect every word placement, every breath.

But I don't let myself indulge in the comfort of Hanna's voice.

I was lonely last night.

Then I wasn't alone anymore, because—

"Good morning, sexy." The woman in my bed sighs softly as she sweeps her eyes over me.

I close my eyes, unable to look at the evidence of what I've done after hearing Hanna's voice. I was wrong. I didn't go to bed with a strange woman.

"Good morning, Vivian."

MAX

Present Day

It's eleven o'clock when my phone buzzes with a text. I'm half asleep and consider ignoring it, but I grab it on the off chance that Hanna is texting or something happened to Claire.

> ***Meredith:*** *You need to come get Claire. I'm so sorry. I'm terrible at this. At everything.*

I frown at my phone and reread the message three times, willing my brain to clear from the fog of sleep. Suddenly, the *not-right* feel of the text clicks in my sleep-riddled mind, and I hit the icon to dial her.

Listening to the ring, I tug on jeans and pull a T-shirt over my head.

"Come on," I growl. I run out to the front of the house to snatch my keys out of the basket and slide into my tennis shoes. Her phone clicks over to voicemail, and I hang up and dial again as I run for the car.

The phone rings ominously in my ear. I start the car and head for Meredith's apartment to the sound of her voice telling me to leave a message. Ugly chills of foreboding wriggle up my spine.

"Pick up the fucking phone, Meredith."

Dialing again gets me the same results. The voicemail is clicking on again when I reach her door. Dropping my phone and keys on the table, I head straight to Claire's room.

My daughter is sleeping in her crib, her little belly rising and falling with the soft breaths of a restful sleep.

I tear out of the room and search for Meredith. Her bedroom is empty, but I find her in the bathroom. She's nude, passed out in a tub full of water, her chin and lips immersed and slowly sinking deeper.

"No!" I lunge for her. Grabbing her under the arms, I yank her from the tub and against my body.

Her eyes flutter open before I can check her pulse. "You'll take good care of her."

"What have you done, Meredith?" The words break, each a crystal dish shattering as it falls from my lips. "What are you *doing*?"

I carry her to the bed, and then I see it. A note placed under an empty bottle of pills.

Dear Claire:

I wish you the best life...

I grab the bedside phone and dial 911.

You are the best thing I've ever made, and I'm sorry I couldn't be—

I throw it across the room, as if reading it makes what she's done real.

"911. What's your emergency, please?"

"I think she's trying to kill herself. I think she overdosed." I grab the bottle and read the name of the prescription painkiller to the operator, and then I give Meredith's address.

"Max," she whispers, her hand settling against my jaw.

Her eyes float closed again, and I hold her against my chest, my fingers on her pulse.

NINETEEN

HANNA

The shrill ring of my phone jars me from a sound sleep. I grope for it in the dark and answer without looking at the display.

"Hello?"

"Hey. It's Max."

I reach across the bed and click on the bedside light. His voice sounds funny. "What happened?"

"I need you to come watch Claire. I wouldn't ask, but it's an emergency and you can get here faster than my mom."

I'm already out of bed, looking for my clothes. "Sure. Of course. Your house?"

"Meredith's apartment. The complex on College, unit 302. They're taking Meredith to the hospital, and I want to follow."

"What happened?"

His breathing is choppy, like maybe he's been running or maybe he's trying not to cry. I can't tell.

"I can't talk about it right now, Hanna."

"I'm on my way."

I dress in the bathroom and am halfway to the door before I consider that Nate might worry if he checks on me in the middle of the night and I'm not here. When I return to the bedroom, a sliver of moonlight is slicing across his bare chest. My heart stops for a minute at the sight of him—strong and solid, yet almost vulnerable in his sleeping state.

I bite my lip, not wanting to wake him up but not wanting to worry him either. Finally, I decide to leave him a note, and I'm heading toward the kitchen for a notepad when I hear him shift in bed.

"I wanted to let you know I'm leaving. I didn't want you to worry."

He sits up and drags a hand over his face before grabbing his phone. "What's going on?"

"Max needs me."

"Want some company?" he asks, his voice that sexy, half-asleep rumble. "Or do you prefer to be alone when you sneak off in the middle of the night with your ex-fiancé?"

I ignore his insinuation and add, "For Claire. I'll— Why are you getting dressed?"

"I'm coming with you." He pulls jeans on over his boxer briefs and then tugs a T-shirt over his head. "I'll drive."

Ten minutes later, we're at Meredith's door. Poor Max is so distraught that he doesn't even notice or care that Nate is with me.

"She's sleeping," Max says. "She'll probably stay asleep until morning, but I need to go." His whole body is a knotted ball of tension.

I swallow back all my questions and whisper, "Go. Claire will be fine."

He pulls me into a hard hug then gives Nate a nod and is out the door.

"What happened?" Nate asks after the door closes behind Max.

"Meredith was rushed to the emergency room. I don't know anything else."

MAX

It's late evening, and she's settled into a room in the psych ward before they let me see her. Hanna has stayed with Claire all day and required no explanations—because that's the kind of friend she is. That's the kind of woman she is.

"Hey," I say softly as I walk into the room.

Meredith is in a hospital gown, an IV in her hand. Her face is washed free of makeup. I can't remember the last time I saw her without at least something on her face, and I'd forgotten that her lashes are nearly as blond as her hair. She looks so fragile, I'm reminded of the girl I loved as a teenager.

"You must think I'm a real idiot," she mutters, staring at her hands.

The truth is, I've felt nothing but guilt since they loaded her into the ambulance and I had to wait for Hanna to arrive. I read the note.

If I'd read it outside of the context of her suicide attempt, I would have seen its contents as self-involved melodrama. But in the context, I see what I've been choosing not to for months. Meredith isn't well. She's depressed and desperate and irrational. And I feel guilty as hell for not noticing the signs. Was I responsible for pushing her to this?

"The doctor said I have postpartum depression." She's still not looking at me. "Which pretty much proves that I totally suck at this mothering thing." She squeezes her eyes shut and tears roll down her cheeks, each one knocking down another piece of my bitterness toward her.

"Why would you say that?"

She swipes at her cheeks with the backs of her hands. "Don't pretend you like me just because you feel sorry for me."

"I think you've done some rotten things, but the way you mother Claire is not one of them."

She sniffs. "I just don't think I was cut out for this mothering stuff. I love her, but some days I feel like..." She stops and takes a breath, and I can't tell if she's shocked by what she was about to say or if she's simply trying to find the courage to say it out loud. "Like I sacrificed my own life the day she was born. And one hundred times worse than missing my life is how shitty I feel about myself for missing it."

"I can help more, you know. Give me custody, and I'll—"

"I was never going to fight you on that. I wouldn't keep her from you." She leans against the back of the inclined bed and deflates. "It's not about the time she takes. It's about not knowing who I am and feeling like no one wants me."

"Can I ask you a question without you getting upset?" I flinch at my own terrible timing. I shouldn't ask an upsetting question to a woman in the psych ward, but she seems like she's in a sharing mood, and I could never bring myself to ask before.

"You want to know if I got pregnant on purpose?"

I draw in a breath. "Yeah." More specifically, did she get pregnant on purpose in the hopes that Will would think it was his? But there's no need to complicate the question yet.

"I really didn't. I wasn't ready for that."

"I wish you would have admitted she was mine sooner."

She shrugs. "I didn't want to admit it to myself."

"Ouch."

"Obviously I was an idiot, and I've realized that now. It never occurred to me that, someday, you wouldn't be there waiting when I needed you again. Then, yesterday, when you told me that you and Hanna had been broken up all summer, I realized that you weren't refusing me just for her." She cuts her gaze to me and then drops it back to her hands. "You really don't want me. Just like him." She doesn't have to clarify for me to know that the *him* she's talking about is Will. This has never stopped being about Will. Not since we were teenagers.

"Meredith..." But I don't know what to say. I can't be with her, and I can't pretend things are different just because she's in here.

"Thank you for being here today, but I'd like it if you left now. I'm tired."

I cross the room, smooth her hair back from her face, and press a kiss to her forehead. "Let me know if you need anything."

HANNA

The only thing that surprises me more than Meredith's agreeing to see me is that I came in the first place.

"Hey," she says when I walk into her room. Her face is scrubbed clean, and she looks almost sweet. "Max said you came over to watch Claire. Thanks for that."

"No problem." I settle into a chair opposite her bed and try to pretend this isn't as awkward as it is. "How are you feeling?"

"Like an idiot. A big, fat idiot." Something like embarrassment passes over her face and she says, "Not that there's anything wrong with being fat or..."

I sigh. Because, really, I'm not fat. Not anymore. I'm pregnant and my belly is heavy with growing twins, but I'm not fat. Maybe I will be again some day, or maybe I'll be able to maintain a smaller size because I'll be spending all my time running after the twins. But Meredith will probably always think of me as the fat girl because that makes her feel better about herself. But the difference between the old Hanna and the woman who stands here today is the understanding that her impression of me has more to do with her than it will *ever* have to do with me.

"I don't like you," Meredith says. "That's never going to change."

The feeling is so damn mutual, but I don't say anything because she's the one in the hospital bed, and unlike her, I don't think saying it out loud is actually going to make me feel any better.

She scowls at me, and when I don't reply, she says, "You honestly have no idea, do you?"

"Why you hate me?" I throw up my hands. "I just know that you were the girl who tripped me in the bleachers at high school football games. You were the one who made *sure* I knew all my body's imperfections. I never did anything to you, and it seemed to me that my existence alone made you hate me."

"Never *did* anything to me?" She rolls her eyes. "My father *adored* you."

I blink at her.

"The American history teacher in high school?"

"I know who he is," I say, shaking my head. "I just don't know what he has to do with anything."

"He was an asshole, you know. Said the cruelest things to my mother, cheated on her"— she raises her gaze to meet mine—"with your mother."

"What? My mother would never—"

"Oh, but she did. She was grieving for her husband and raising five girls on her own, and my father was the shoulder to cry on." She releases a long, slow breath. "She didn't care whose family she was destroying when she slept with him. She didn't care how my mother would feel when he decided he couldn't be with her anymore because he loved Gretchen too much. It was all so inconsequential to her, and after tearing apart my family, she cast him aside like he was nothing. Like mother, like daughter, I guess."

"I didn't tear apart your family." I can't speak to her accusations about my mother, but this I know for sure. "You weren't even *with* Max when he started dating me."

"You know what I got to hear that year he was fucking around with your mom? You were in his history class, and I was out of cosmetology school and trying to build my client list. *'Why can't you be more like Hanna? Why can't you be smart like her? Why can't you be sweet like her? Why do you have to be such a dumb slut?'* You were everything he wanted in a daughter, and I was everything he was ashamed of."

"Meredith, I had no idea." Suddenly, all of her cruelty makes a little sense. It's not okay, and she's still a bad person, but sometimes badness is easier to take when you understand the *why* behind it.

"Because you're so self-involved you can't see beyond your own nose." She releases her breath in a huff. "Max and Claire and I could be happy, you know. If it weren't for you."

"You didn't want him, Meredith. You had your chance." But her words still burn because they're probably true.

Just like Vivian was right when she said I would be standing in the way of her, Nate, and Collin being a family. I'm not sure if I get a family of my own or if I'm doomed to ruin everyone else's.

"You're no better than me. Look at you, playing house with that rocker while Max just waits for you. You think Nate Crane is going to move to New Hope?"

My stomach turns sour at the question. I already know the answer, and just because I understand why he can't doesn't make it hurt any less. I want the guy who will turn his world inside out for me.

No. I don't. Max was that guy. What I want is *Nate* to be the guy who will turn his world inside out for me. And it's not fair for me to want it.

"You really think he ever stopped fucking his actress?" she adds.

"Don't," I growl.

"Whatever. *I* didn't push you down the stairs," Meredith says quietly. "I don't care for you, and I don't think you deserve Max, but I would never intentionally injure someone that badly."

I take a breath and nod, but I don't apologize. Considering all she's done and said to me, I don't think my suspicion was unreasonable.

"But I wasn't the last person there that night either."

That gets my attention and I look up at her.

She's frowning. "I only remember because I didn't know about Nate then, but I was convinced you were sleeping around on Max, and this guy came up the stairs."

"What guy?"

She shrugs. "He kind of looked like Fabio, I guess."

My breath catches. "Was anyone with him?"

She shrugs. "We were in your apartment talking—fighting—and then you looked out your window and the Fabio guy was out there. You said you needed me to go because you had company." She frowns for a minute. "I assumed you knew who it was. Actually"—she shakes her head—"I assumed it was your lover—whoever you were cheating on Max with."

"I have to go," I whisper, grabbing my purse. "Thank you for telling me."

"Hanna," she calls as I reach for the door. "You're lucky. Anyone who receives Max's love is lucky."

I face the door and close my eyes for a moment. "I know."

TWENTY

HANNA

"I need to talk to you," I say.

Nate's in his room, packing his suitcase. He's heading back to California for Christmas. It only makes sense that he'd spend Christmas with Collin since this is the last Christmas that he won't have to choose between his children.

He looks up from his luggage and grins at me. He's seemed so damn happy lately, and I'm about to ruin everything by telling him what I suspect.

He throws some socks into the luggage and opens his arms for me. "Come here."

I step forward and let him wrap me in his arms. For a moment, I close my eyes and revel in the comfort of his nearness, his warmth, and his scent.

"Nix has never thought I fell down the stairs."

Nate straightens and pulls back to look at my face. "What does she think happened, then?"

"She's always believed I was pushed."

I feel his whole body tense and his arms tighten around me. "Who the fuck would do that?"

"That's what I've been trying to figure out."

"Shit, Hanna. Someone almost killed you and you haven't said a word about it to me? What if they're still out there? What if—"

"I'm telling you now."

He relaxes a bit and pulls my head against his chest. "I'm sorry. I just can't handle the idea of anyone hurting you."

I swallow. "I knew you'd feel that way."

"Do you remember anything? Has any of that day come back to you?"

"Not really." I step back—out of his arms so I can look at his face while I talk. "But some memories from the days before have, and I think I know who pushed me."

He raises a brow, and I can tell he has no idea why it's taking me so long to spit it out.

"I think Vivian did it."

He actually smiles. Smiles. "That's funny. What else ya got?"

I shake my head. "I'm serious. She wanted me out of your life. She came here specifically to ask me to let her have a chance with you."

His face has gone deadly serious. "That's a far cry from pushing you down the stairs."

"Listen, I never thought about it until today, but when she was in town last time, I went over to Asher's, and you and Vivian were fighting in the basement. Drake was at the top of the stairs and he said that, the last time he saw me, I was wearing Max's ring. Which means they must have been here the day of the accident."

"Vivian didn't push you down the stairs. She wouldn't do that." He drags a hand through his hair and cracks a sardonic smile. "Christ, have you seen the woman? She's half your size."

I wince. "Thanks."

"Jesus, Hanna. Seriously? You're accusing a sweet, loving woman of a serious crime and you're going to take offense to a reference to your size differences?"

"You don't have any idea how hard it was for me to tell you this," I whisper.

"She didn't do it, so let it go."

"Meredith was here that day too," I say.

"Well, *there's* a more likely suspect."

"She said I asked her to leave when a guy who looked like Fabio showed up at my apartment." When he looks at me blankly, I say, "Drake. Drake looks like Fabio in his romance cover days, and everyone knows Vivian doesn't go anywhere without Drake."

"So you're saying Vivian wanted you away from me so badly that she came to your apartment and, when she saw you were wearing his ring, she pushed you down the stairs?" He shakes his head. "Come on, Hanna. That doesn't even make sense."

"I just know she wanted me away from you. She told me as much."

"Of course she did. Do I wish she wouldn't have come here and asked you to stay away? Sure, but that's not *that* unreasonable. She wanted me back. She wanted our family back together. That's no crime."

"No. But pushing me down the stairs is."

He rubs the back of his neck. "Let it go. Please. It wasn't her."

"How do you know that? How do you *know*?"

"Other than the fact that I've known her most of my life and I know better than anyone that she's not capable of hurting someone like that?"

"Yeah. Other than that."

"She was in London the day of your accident. She didn't push you down the fucking stairs."

"What if she just *told* you she was in London? What if that was her cover because she was really here trying to make me forget—"

"I know," he says, and his words are so quiet that I finally believe him. "I know because she was in my bed."

My heart plummets because surely he doesn't mean… *"You really think he ever stopped fucking his actress?"* Of course that's what I thought. Why would I have believed anything else when I was so convinced I was the one he wanted?

"What?"

"You'd cut me out of your life and wouldn't even talk to me about it."

"So you took her to London with you?"

"It wasn't like that."

"What was it like, then? You took my virginity, told me you

wanted me to leave Max for you, and by the way, a future with you meant a life in LA with no kids. And then, while I went home to search my heart and figure out if I could sacrifice everything I ever wanted for you, while I fought every instinct that said I should be with you no matter the cost, you were in London with your ex, trying to make sure you really meant the very fucking little you promised me. Fuck you, Nate. *Fuck. You.*"

"You chose him, Hanna." His shoulders sag and he studies me for a beat. "He's the one you were so sure was right for you. I'm just the guy who knocked you up."

We stare at each other, and my heart hurts so badly that I expect it to stop working at any minute. The silence pulses around us like an angry, living thing.

"I have to leave. Collin's expecting me tonight."

"Nate…"

"I have to leave. You and I…" He shrugs, and I feel like pieces of my heart have fallen into my stomach and are decomposing inside me. "Vivian's always going to be part of my life because Collin's always going to be part of my life. And you will always be a part of my life too. We're going to figure this out."

"That's what you keep saying."

Nate leaves the room, suitcase in hand. I feel broken and empty.

I need to go to the bakery. With the holiday rush, I have plenty there to keep me busy, and if the simple chemistry of baking can't busy my mind, nothing can.

I head downstairs to change. I'm halfway down the hallway when I hear footsteps behind me.

"Hanna."

Then Nate is spinning me around and pressing his mouth against mine. I'm so scared this is goodbye. I cling to him as I kiss him back. Our mouths are open, greedy, and demanding, and when he pulls back, he wipes a tear from my cheek.

"I'm sorry," he whispers. "I'm sorry I couldn't let you go. I'm sorry I couldn't keep my promise not to fight for you. Maybe you'd be better with him. He's the better guy, but I'm the *right* guy and you're *mine*."

"What about her?" I ask. "Are you sorry for sleeping with her?"

He shakes his head. "I don't even remember it. I remember her showing up. I was lonely. I was pissed. I missed you more than I ever thought I could miss someone. She showed up in the bar, and I wasn't alone anymore."

"So you slept with her."

"I thought I'd lost you. I got drunk. And I woke up in bed with her."

"You slept with her," I repeat.

His eyes meet mine. "Yeah. I slept with her."

I nod, and hot tears roll out of the corners of my eyes. "Do you still love her?"

"Not the way I love you."

"Do you still love her?" I am a broken record.

"She's the mother of my son. I'll always love her."

Vivian was right. I'm stealing something from him by being in his life. Would he even be here right now if it weren't for these babies?

"Go to her."

"Hanna, it's not like that," he growls.

"I'm not walking away," I tell him. "I'm letting you go."

"The fuck you are. I won't let you." He squeezes my shoulders and presses his mouth to mine, but I don't open under him this time. I'm stronger now. If only I'd been stronger sooner.

"You are too good of a father to miss Christmas with Collin just so you can stay here and fight with me."

"Come with me." He shakes his head. "I'm not asking you to move. Just come for the holiday. Janelle will arrange for someone to cover the bakery."

"We both know I don't belong there."

"Don't do this, Hanna. I'm sorry I didn't tell you about London sooner, but I hardly had you. I couldn't risk losing you."

"Tell me something." I force a full breath into my lungs. "If you hadn't met me, would you be with her now?"

He pales. "Don't make me answer that."

The kitchen clock ticks, and on the street, a snow plow's blade scrapes the street.

"But we both already know the answer," I say. "Merry

Christmas, Nate. Give Collin a hug for me."

I walk away from him before my strength dissolves, and I shut and lock my bedroom door behind me. Time runs away from me. Minutes, hours, seconds—everything is meaningless but the measure of his steps against the floorboards toward my room, the space of the silence as he waits by my door, and the creak of the front door opening and closing.

I don't change clothes and I don't go to the bakery. I crawl into bed, curl onto my side, and fall asleep.

My bed feels cold. Empty. I reach for Nate and grasp at air. Slowly, I reorient myself, remember the argument, curl into myself at the memory of his confession.

"I thought I'd lost you."

My stomach hurts—aches—with grief.

I gasp and put my hand to my belly, where the cramps that woke me are making my whole core ache. Not so different than the cramps I got with my periods, the pain is low in my pelvis and wraps around to my lower back.

"No," I whisper, but there's no one here to hear the word. I'm afraid to move, but I know I have to. I grab my phone from the end table and pull up my contacts list.

A sob lodges in my throat when I see Nate's name, but he should be in California by now. I scroll past his name and dial Nix.

NATE

Drake opens the door when I arrive at Vivian's and inclines his chin. "Collin's already sleeping."

I'm lunging for him before I know what I'm doing—pressing him against the wall with my hand at his neck. "What did you do to her?" Because Vivian was in London with me, but I have no idea where Drake was that day. I always assumed he was somewhere in London—he never strays far from Vivian's side—but he could very well have been in New Hope assaulting the woman I love in some misguided attempt to protect the woman *he* loves.

"To whom?" he grunts. He barely seems fazed by the fact that I have him against the wall.

"Nathaniel, what are you doing?" Vivian asks behind me. "Let him go."

"What did you do to Hanna?"

Drake lifts a brow and points to his neck, indicating that he won't talk until I release him.

"You were there the day of the accident," I say, and I back up because I need to know what happened. "You saw her with the ring on."

Drake rubs his neck and looks to Vivian.

She nods. "Tell him."

"When Viv went to London, I went to New Hope to talk to Hanna one more time."

"If you hurt her," I growl, "I'll fucking kill you."

"No, you won't," Vivian snaps.

"I didn't hurt her." Drake throws up his hands. "Why would I have wanted to do that? I was just there to find out what she'd decided, and she was wearing that local boy's ring."

I flinch. "Did she ever say why?" I don't want it to matter to me. It shouldn't matter if I have her now. But it does.

"She said that she loved him," Vivian says, talking for Drake. "That she wanted to marry Max, and it was her final decision."

I push past them and into the living room and collapse on the couch. My gut aches, and I feel like I'm seconds from losing the tequila I had on the plane.

"I thought you knew," Vivian says behind me.

I rest my head in my hands. Of course I did. She was wearing his ring. My own damn sister said Hanna was leaning in that direction.

"But I didn't believe. Jesus. I don't know why it matters so much, but I needed to believe she'd choose me."

"Maybe she would have," she says softly. "I did something

terrible."

I stiffen. I've known since the beginning of this conversation that something was coming. "Hanna?"

She nods. "I didn't want you getting hurt. I'd never seen you like this. I was afraid she was just some money-grubbing, celebrity-chasing…"

When Viv's eyes meet mine, I can see I don't have to explain. She knows now that Hanna isn't any of those things. "What did you do?"

"I went to New Hope and informed her I was still in love with you."

"So I hear."

She chews on her bottom lip and shakes her head. "I told her she was standing in the way of a *family*. That if she would move aside, you would finally have the thing you want most. What you need most."

"When?" My voice is hard.

Her face crumbles and she shakes her head. "I'm so sorry, Nate. I didn't realize how good she is or how very much you love her."

"When was this, Viv?"

She shrugs. "Back in August. Before I met you in London."

Before the accident. Before she put on Max's ring. Before I fucked up.

"Fuck," I mutter, dragging a hand through my hair. No wonder.

"She's lucky," she says to her wine. "I would have killed to have you look at me just once the way you look at her."

"Why didn't you ever tell me how you felt? Years ago, before your marriage, before Hanna?" I wait for her to look at me, but she stays focused on her wine, looking for all the answers there.

"I thought you didn't love me. I thought the problem was *me*, so I pushed you away. You don't let people in. You know that? You and Janelle are so close, but you shut the rest of the world out. When I realized it wasn't just me, I thought it was too late."

"I never meant to shut you out."

"You changed last summer. You smiled more. You'd been living like a zombie for years and suddenly you were awake. You were happier, and I thought we could make it work." Finally, she brings her eyes to mine. "By the time I realized *she* was the reason, it was too late. Sure, I was still married, but mentally, I'd moved on with you."

"Dammit, Viv. I never meant for you to dissolve your marriage for me."

"I had to. If I was willing to leave him for you, I shouldn't have been with him at all." She takes a sip of her wine, and her sip turns to a long drink until the glass is nearly empty.

"Tell me what I can do."

"Give me physical custody of Collin," I reply without hesitation. "Let me take him to New Hope to live with me."

She draws in a shaky breath. "I won't have half the country between me and my son."

"Don't make me fight you, Viv. I've learned the hard way I need to fight for what I want—for who I love."

HANNA

"The good news," Nix says as she scans the monitors beside the bed, "is that the medicine made the contractions stop."

I stare at the monitors, unsure what they all mean but too scared that, if I look away, they'll stop their beeping and wiggling and something terrible will happen to my babies.

"What's the bad news?" I whisper.

Liz squeezes my hand.

When I called Nix, she told me to have Nate drive me to Labor and Delivery. I called Liz and had her bring me. I don't think she's taken a full breath since we arrived. She's not the only one.

"The bad news," Nix says, "is that you're a centimeter dilated and you're looking at bed rest for the remainder of your pregnancy."

I dare to take my eyes off the monitors to look at Nix. "Bed rest? That's it?"

Nix sighs. "Well, this will all be up to your perinatologist, so it's just speculation on my part, but I imagine they'll keep you here to monitor you for a couple of days. If the medicine appears to be working and keeping your contractions at bay, they'll continue with it, put you on strict bed rest, and keep a careful eye on you. We want those babies to stay in there as long as they can."

The room is tense with the words she's not saying: the prognosis for twins born at twenty weeks' gestation is not a good one.

Liz looks like she might lose it and start crying any minute. "Do you think this is because of her fall?"

"I don't know," Nix says. "But that's highly unlikely. If that fall was going to create a problem, I imagine we would have seen it early on. Or we would have never known about the pregnancy."

My eyes are back on the monitors, but I feel Nix's hand on my shoulder.

"Try not to worry too much about why. Just rest. And get a hold of Nate. He'll want to know."

She shuts off the lights on her way out and leaves Liz and me in the glow of the light trickling in from the bathroom.

"Do you want me to call him?" Liz asks.

I shake my head, but I don't mean no. I just mean that I don't know. He's in California to spend Christmas with Collin, and I don't want to ruin that.

"He's upset with me," I finally admit. "I told him I thought Vivian pushed me down the stairs. And he told me she couldn't have because she was in London." I swallow. "In bed with him."

Liz gasps and chokes a little, and when I turn my head to look at her, her face is red and splotchy and she's crying.

"It's okay," I say. "I don't blame him."

She shakes her head. "I didn't know you really believed someone pushed you."

I shrug. "I don't know what I believe anymore."

"No one pushed you," she whispers. "Not intentionally at least." Then she sinks to her knees and rests her head on the side of my bed. "I'm so sorry."

"Liz?" Panic lodges in my throat. "Liz, what's wrong?"

"I'm so sorry," she repeats. "You're the most important person in my world, and I would never hurt you on purpose."

Oh my God. "What happened, Liz?"

She lifts her head and draws in a ragged breath. "The day of the accident, Sam called me and said you'd met with him. He said he was worried about you and that maybe you were about to rush into a marriage you weren't ready for." She pushes herself off her haunches and paces the room. "Of course, I didn't know anything about Max proposing at the beginning of the summer, and the idea of you getting married was new to me. And terrifying. You'd pulled away from me completely. You'd become a shell of your former self—exercised-obsessed and quiet and secretive—and in my mind, that was all associated with Max. I thought he made you like that. I thought that, if you married him, I'd lose you forever."

I force myself to steady my breathing. I know what's coming.

"I came up to your apartment to see if what Sam said was true and to try to talk you out of rushing into it. You met me on the balcony and you had a puffy lip and a swollen eye. You wouldn't tell me what those were from, and you were wearing the ring." She stops pacing and lifts her eyes to mine. "I demanded that you take it off. I'm your twin sister, and I didn't even know he'd proposed, and you were wearing his ring, telling me that I needed to trust you. You were doing the right thing, you said. But to me, it was all wrong, and I wanted my sister back. I tried to take the ring off you myself. I was desperate. I felt like it had you under some spell or something and if I could get it off your finger…"

"And I didn't want you to take it," I say softly.

"I don't even know how it happened. I had your hand and you were yanking away from me, and you told me to let go, said I was hurting you, and I did. But your back was to the stairs and somehow you lost your balance and fell." Tears spill down her cheeks. "I called 911 and got you to the hospital, and it was so much more terrible than I ever would have imagined a fall like that could be. I was terrified I was going to lose you. And then, when I didn't, I couldn't bring myself to tell you the truth because I finally had my sister back. I am so sorry."

"It was an accident, Liz."

"It was my fault."

"It was an *accident*," I repeat. But my mind is spinning and I wonder what would have happened if I hadn't taken that fall. Was I planning on telling Max about Nate? And when would I have learned about the pregnancy?

"Can I get you anything?" she asks. "Anything at all? Should I call him?"

"Don't call Nate."

"He'll come," she says. "He loves you."

I nod, and a salty tear runs into my mouth. "He does."

What was it he said to me the day we made love? *"I love you, and I'm afraid you're going to ruin your life because of it."* Turns out, it wasn't my life he needed to worry about.

TWENTY-ONE

MAX

She looks terrified and she's staring at the babies' heart-rate monitors like their hearts might stop beating if she turns away.

"She's doing great," Liz says, patting Hanna's arm. "No more contractions since they started her on the meds. Babies are healthy and strong. Now we just have to keep them cooking for a while longer."

"Have you called Nate?" I ask Hanna.

Liz speaks before Hanna can reply—or maybe she just knows she won't. "He's spending Christmas with his son."

"He can't be in both places at once," Hanna murmurs, almost to herself.

Liz frowns, exhaustion marking her features, but she pats Hanna's arm again. "He'd be here if he knew. Someone's being stubborn."

"Have you been here all day?" I ask Liz.

She nods. "It's no big deal. She's my sister."

"Take a break. I'll stay with her for a while. She won't be alone."

Relief lightens her smile. "Thanks."

"I'm so scared," Hanna whispers when Liz is gone. "I don't know if I can do this."

I sink into the chair between her bed and the monitors so she'll see me while we talk without having to take her attention completely off the graphs of the babies' heartbeats. "Everything looks good. They can do amazing things to stop preterm labor."

"It's not that. It's that I don't know the first thing about being a mom."

Taking her hand, I squeeze her fingers. "You're going to be amazing."

"I'm scared to do this alone."

"You won't be alone. We're all here for you. You know that."

A tear escapes her eye and rolls onto the pillow. "I'm so sorry for what I put you through."

My heart squeezes so hard and tight and painful that I can hardly breathe. "Hanna..."

"I am. You sacrificed everything for me, and how did I repay you? By doubting you? By stringing you along? By falling in love with another man? Will you ever be able to forgive me?"

"I will." I sigh and shake my head. "I already have."

"You, Maximilian Hallowell, are an amazing man, and someday, you're going to make some lucky woman very happy."

"You just say the word and it can be you." I don't even care that I sound desperate. It's the truth, and I need to know she understands.

"I'm in love with Nate," she says simply.

"Are you going to be with him? You deserve commitment, marriage, happily ever after."

"I don't know." She lifts her eyes to meet mine, and there's more determination there than I've ever seen. "But what will or won't happen doesn't change that my heart is his, and I never should have asked you to settle for me when I knew that was true."

"For me, it wouldn't have been settling."

HANNA

"Wowee!" Granny says, cocking her head at Liz. "You are so

conflicted. If you could see your aura now."

Liz rolls her eyes. "I'm going to go clean up dinner."

"I'll help," Maggie says.

Mom looks at me. "Let's get you back to bed."

They let me out of the hospital this morning, and Mom insisted we hold Christmas Eve dinner at my house. I didn't even object. The idea of spending Christmas alone and stuck in bed is miserable. If I can't have Nate, all I want is to be by my family.

Liz and Maggie take stacks of dishes into the kitchen and quietly begin cleaning up, and Mom helps me out of the recliner they dragged into the dining room for me.

"I want to go to the living room," I tell her.

She props me up on the couch, positioning pillows to make it more comfortable. Then she sits in the chair across from me.

"Mom, I need to confess something," I say after a long silence.

"The only one you need to confess to is Jesus, Hanna, but you go down and talk to Father Douglas, and I have no doubt you'll find the forgiveness you seek."

I stifle an eye roll and take a deep breath. "I never wanted to marry Max for the right reasons. A girl should put on a man's ring when she knows he's the one she wants to be with. But I wasn't thinking about who *I* wanted. I was just trying to find a way that everyone could be happy."

"That sounds like you," she says with a sigh. She picks up her bag from beside the chair and pulls her latest knitting project from it. "I just hate to see you alone."

I want to tell her that I'm not alone. That I have Nate. But I'm not sure I'm okay with sacrificing his happiness for my own.

"Did you sleep with Meredith's dad?"

Mom's hands freeze in the middle of a stitch, and I have to remind myself to breathe while I wait for her answer. She starts working again without looking at me. "I never cheated on your father. Malcolm and I were friends." She sighs and finally lifts her head to meet my eyes. "You girls think I'm crazy for wanting you to get married, but you don't know how difficult it is to live in this world without a man."

I cross my arms and wait for her to finish, but my stomach

hurts.

"I miss your father so much," she whispers, and her eyes fill with tears. "Not only because he was my husband and the father to my children. He took care of things. Life was so much easier when he was around, and when he left, I didn't know how to do anything. I'd never paid the bills or balanced the checkbook. I'd never changed my own wiper blades. I never realized just how much your father took care of me until he was gone, and Malcolm was a friend, and he helped me with those little things. I had no idea he thought our relationship was more than friendship until he left his wife. And we tried for a while, but then I saw his true colors and…" She sighs. "Good men aren't so easy to find, you know."

"Mom, if you didn't know how to do any of those things, wouldn't you want your daughters to wait on marriage? To be single and independent for a while first?"

She gives me a hard look then stands to take my hand in hers. "*Single* and *independent* are words women use to make themselves feel better about being *lonely* and *overwhelmed*. I want all of my girls to marry a good man and have a good life. I don't think that makes me a bad person."

"We can't just marry anyone and have what you had with Dad," I say softly.

Her smile is sad, a little hopeful. "But Max would give you that. You'd never be alone and you'd always have someone at your side to help you through the tough days."

"I already have lots of people to help me through the tough days." I shift our hands so mine is squeezing hers, and her shoulders rise on her inhale. "And I count you among them."

She drops her gaze to our joined hands. "I know I'm far from perfect. Some days, I feel like I've failed each of you girls in a different way."

"You didn't *fail* me, Mom. I just…"

"You just felt like I wouldn't love you if you weren't thin. That sounds like a failure to me."

"No," I say firmly. "I knew you'd always love me. You pressured me to lose weight, to be thin, that's true. But I knew you wanted the best for me, and I never doubted that you loved me."

She sniffs and forces a smile. "If you want to raise these babies on your own, I will support you. Whatever you need, whatever my grandchildren need. You just say the word."

I don't reply because my eyes are glued to my open front door, and the tall, dark-haired man with a little boy in his arms.

NATE

"Hanna!" Collin calls when he spots her. I put him down, and he scurries across the foyer and into the living room. "How are my sibwings?"

"Sib*lings*," I correct, but then I close my mouth because Collin's gently cupping his hands over Hanna's rounded belly, and the vision brings me more joy than I can fit in my heart. She's lying on the couch, propped up with pillows behind her head and under her hips, and I want to scoop her into my arms and hold her close.

"They're good, Collin," Hanna answers, her eyes on me. "Did Liz call you?"

"No." I shed my coat and walk into the living room to crouch down beside my son.

"Max?" she asks.

"No."

Her breath catches as I place my hands next to Collin's. As if in greeting, a baby kicks, then the other.

"I feel them!" Collin says with wide eyes.

I lift my eyes to Hanna's and a smile stretches across my face. "Me too."

"Who told you, then?" she asks. "Why are you here?"

"I'm here because I want to spend Christmas with the woman I love."

At the sound of a sharp inhale, I tear my eyes away from Hanna's face and look up at her mother.

"You two need a minute," she says. She offers her hand to my son. "Collin, is it? You want to see if we can find any Christmas cookies in Hanna's kitchen?"

"Yeah!" He takes her hand, and Hanna's mom winks at me as they leave the room.

"I started having contractions the night you left. But I went to the hospital, and they put me on medicine to make them stop."

Her admission robs me of my breath, and I rest my cheek on her stomach. "Why didn't you call me?"

"I should have. I'm trying to figure out how to ask for what I need." She shakes her head. "I'm not very good at it. I've spent my whole life trying to make everyone else happy, and I'm starting to think that's not healthy."

I raise a brow. "Ya think?"

She shrugs. "The only reason I was in St. Louis the night we met was because I knew Maggie wanted me there. So it's not a terrible trait."

I brush her hair behind her ear. I want to kiss her, to hold her until the racing in my chest subsides and I know she's okay. "Not terrible," I agree. "But you aren't always so good at knowing what makes people happy."

"What do you mean by that?"

I draw a finger down her jaw, count the freckles across the bridge of her nose, memorize the exact shade of the pink of her lips. "You asked me if I would be with Vivian if I'd never met you. And the answer is *yes*. I'm sure I would be."

"Oh," she whispers. "I guess I knew that already."

"But, you see, you didn't ask the right question. Ask me if I would be happier if I'd never met you, Hanna. Ask me if a life with Collin's mother would have made me feel alive the way loving you makes me feel. Ask me if I'd take back our time together, even if you'd chosen Max."

I lean my head against hers, and she swallows so hard I can hear it. "I only thought everyone would be happier if I married him."

"Would *you* have been happier?"

She shakes her head. "No. Anyone paying attention would know you're the one for me. I gave you what I would never give Max—and not just my body. I trusted you like I never trusted him, needed you like I never needed him. I chose him for everyone but myself, but I *wanted* you."

She doesn't say any more because I'm kissing her—my mouth open over hers, my hands in her hair, my heart hers to keep.

I want to hold her until there's nothing in the world but us. I want to chase away the ugliness and protect her from any more hurt. But I know I can't, so I pour all of my love and hope into this one kiss.

She lifts slightly off the couch, her hand grazing my chest. "I feel empty when you're gone."

I cup her face in my hand and kiss her again. She's so damn sweet and perfect, and I love the feel of her tongue against mine, the way she moans into my mouth when I deepen the kiss.

"Hey now!"

Liz's voice pulls me from the kiss, and I lift my head to glare at her.

"The doctor very clearly said no shopping, no sports, no *sex*. Orgasms are an even bigger no-no, so stop while you're ahead."

I look to Hanna, who nods. "It's true. No sex until it's safe for the babies to be born."

I cock a brow and say, "Looks like Aunt Liz is going to need to do a lot of babysitting so we can make up for lost time after they're born."

Hanna smacks me in the chest, but she's grinning.

"I'd be happy to," Liz says.

"Me too," another woman calls. The petite brunette steps into the room and offers me her hand. "I'm Hanna's oldest sister, Krystal. Nice to meet you."

I shake her hand and nod. "Nice to meet you too."

"Krystal lived in Florida for a while," Hanna explains, "but she just moved back home, and she's going to run the bakery for me while I'm on bed rest. Then, when the babies are old enough for me to go back, she's going to run the front for me."

"I'm tough to replace," Liz says, "but seeing as how Krystal doesn't loathe mornings like I do, she might be a better fit."

One by one, everyone joins us in the living room, talking and laughing around the Christmas tree. After putting Collin to bed upstairs and promising him that Santa will know where to find him, I sit on the couch with Hanna's head in my lap and her family gathered around us. No wonder she didn't want to leave this place. It's warm and loving and comfortable. It's home.

HANNA

I hear the television click off, and when I open my eyes, my head is in Nate's lap. "Did everyone leave?"

"A couple of hours ago." He's watching me, tenderness in his eyes. He tucks a lock of hair behind my ear and strokes my cheek.

"What are you looking at?" I ask quietly.

"My angel. My heart."

My throat grows thick. "I love you." Tears spill onto my cheeks as his hand settles on my belly. "I love you so much."

"Let me live here with you."

"You don't have to do that. We'll make it work. Somehow." I swallow. "Like you said, we'll figure it out."

"Yeah, but I'm a selfish bastard who gets what he wants. I want to live here with you. I want to marry you and raise these babies by your side." He traces my lips with his thumb. "I want to make love to you every night and cook for you. Say yes," he says softly, and his Adam's apple bobs as he swallows hard. "Say you'll marry me and be my family."

My chest aches with hope and happiness and...guilt. "What about Collin?"

He looks to the stairs then back at me. "He likes the room he's sleeping in tonight, though, to be fair, it won't look nearly so tidy when we move his toys in." He smiles. "Vivian doesn't want to raise him in LA, so I've asked her to raise him here."

"And she agreed?"

He shrugs. "Not at first—she really is very jealous of you—but Drake talked her into it. Collin loves it here. He loves seeing Asher and playing by the river. She knows it would be good for him. She's going to start looking to relocate to Indiana after the holidays."

"Wow. That's amazing."

"You still haven't answered me, woman."

I grin. "I made a promise to myself that I wouldn't rush into any engagements until after the babies are born. But you have my permission to ask again then."

"That's fine," he says. He presses a kiss to my ear then whispers, "As long as you're planning on saying yes."

TWENTY-TWO

MAX

Meredith closes Claire's bedroom door softly behind her as she joins me in the living room. She's dressed for work in a tight black skirt and bright-colored, cleavage-showing sweater. Her hair is styled sleek and smooth, and her makeup is applied with its usual attention. But she looks tired. Drained.

The emotional exhaustion I see in her eyes slingshots me back to our teenage years, when she hid her hurt from the world and I thought I could save her.

"Come here," I whisper, opening my arms.

Her face crumples and she runs into my arms and buries her face in my chest. She wraps her arms tightly around my back, and I can't tell if she's crying or just breathing me in.

I run my hand over her hair and sigh. "I'm sorry I accused you of pushing Hanna. When I think of someone trying to hurt her, I lose my mind a little."

She pulls out of my arms and looks at the floor. Her tears left smudges of eye makeup under her eyes. "I kind of earned it by being such a bitch. I just couldn't accept that you'd rather be with her than me."

I tilt her chin up so she's looking at me. "And you'd rather be with William Bailey than with me." When she flinches, I add, "What if I told you we could be together and the next day Will said *he* wanted to be with you. Be honest here, Mer. You'd drop me in a second." She doesn't deny it, and I sigh and pull her against my chest again. "You deserve to be head over heels for the guy you end up with. And he should be head over heels for you. Don't settle for someone because you don't want to be alone."

"I don't know how to be head over heels for anyone but Will," she whispers. "And guys don't love me like that. You're the only one who ever did, and now you hate me."

"You've pissed me off enough times, but I don't hate you. I couldn't."

She tilts her face to mine and her gaze locks on to my lips.

Once upon a time, these were my favorite moments with Meredith—the moments when she dropped her defenses and let me in. And if I hadn't changed, I would drop my mouth to hers and kiss her softly. She'd turn it wild before I'd gotten my fill of her taste, and we'd end up naked and sweaty on the couch.

But I'm not that guy anymore, so I kiss her cheek before stepping back.

"Still holding out for Hanna?" she asks, but there's no sign of the bitterness that usually infects her voice on the topic of my once-fiancée.

"That ship's sailed, unfortunately."

"Maybe not. She's not in any rush to commit to the rocker, so there may be a chance for you two."

I collapse on the couch and lean against the headrest so I'm looking at the ceiling. "I don't think so. I think some relationships start out wildly unbalanced and they're doomed to try to survive on this rickety teeter-totter. That's the way it was for Hanna and me. I was always trying to make up for the beginning of our relationship—for not wanting her at the beginning, for dating her for the wrong reasons and taking so long to realize how great she was. We were off-balance from the start, and I spent every day of our relationship trying to catch my balance so I wouldn't lose her."

Meredith sinks onto the couch beside me and rests her head on my shoulder. "You mean by doing things like buying her a bakery you really couldn't afford?"

"Yeah. Like that." My stomach aches to admit this. "I think I knew I was losing her even before you shared those texts with her. She always held back part of herself, and she was so good and sweet I was greedy for her to let me in, even in those moments when things were good. Then you sent her those texts, and it's been wildly teetering ever since."

She stiffens beside me. "Will you ever be able to forgive me for that?"

"It was a really bitchy thing to do. It hurt Hanna and it hurt me." I wrap my arm around her shoulders. "And I think it hurt you too."

"I know my depression isn't an excuse, but I really wasn't seeing clearly. I'd like to think I wouldn't have done anything that terrible if I'd been in my right mind."

"You're going to spend the rest of your life alone if you keep acting like that," I say softly. Not to be an ass, but she needs to know. "Every bitter, angry thing you do and say alienates you a little more."

"And makes me a little more like my father." The words are so quiet I probably wouldn't have made them out if I weren't thinking the same thing.

"Go to Paris. Start fresh. Be the Meredith *I* knew. The one who'd sneak into bed with me and whisper about her dreams for the future."

"I don't know what happened to her."

"So find her. Who knows? Maybe you'll meet the love of your life in the process."

She sits up, tilts her head, and studies me. "And what about you?"

I shrug. "I've got Claire. Right now, she's the love of my life."

She throws her hand over her mouth and her eyes fill with tears. "I'm so glad she has you," she manages, tears rolling onto her cheeks, "since her mom is so screwed up."

She pushes off the couch and grabs her purse off the kitchen table. I follow her to the door, but when I open it, she faces me again. "I am so sorry for being the reason things didn't work out with Hanna. So sorry. If I could go back…"

I take her hand and squeeze her fingers. "If we hadn't already been off-balance, anything you did or said wouldn't have mattered. It took seeing her with Nate to understand that. They're steady. Despite…everything. When the world throws them for a loop, they're fine as soon as they get their feet on the ground."

She nods and looks to the door of Claire's bedroom. "Tell her every day how much I love her. Tell her I'm coming back for her. I don't want her to feel…" She presses her fingers to her lips. "Stupid antidepressant clearly isn't working," she says, half smiling as more tears roll down her cheeks.

"I think they're working just fine. And you don't need to worry. I'll tell her. Every day."

HANNA

"This is the cutest nursery ever," Liz says. She's adorable with her blond curls pulled into a high ponytail, smudges of red paint on her cheek.

I can't disagree. I love everything about the nursery. The walls are a pale yellow with a bold, red accent wall. We used primary colors and found gender-neutral bed sets with colorful zoo animals.

"You think it'll be two girls or two boys or a boy and a girl?"

I shrug.

"I know, I know! We just want them to be healthy, but part of me is hoping it'll be two little girls." She slings her arm over my shoulder and eyes my belly. "Or not so little," she teases. "I'm surprised I got to come over tonight, honestly. Nate hasn't taken his hands off you since the doctor told him it was safe to have sex."

I bite back a grin then sigh. Having Nate in my house the last four months has been amazing. Vivian and Drake bought a house in a ritzy little area outside of Indianapolis, not a bad drive from New Hope, and Collin stays with us during the week and stays with them on the weekends.

Everything was going so well that they took me off complete bed rest by thirty weeks, but only last week, when I hit the thirty-seven-week mark, were we released to have sex again. If I was worried about my enormous belly standing between me and Nate being intimate, I needn't have. He's plenty creative when it counts.

The thought sends a buzz of anticipation through me. I shift uncomfortably and move away from Liz to sit in the glider rocker Nate bought for the nursery. So many thoughtful touches for a man who never wanted more children. Or who told himself that he didn't want any more children. My heart pinches a bit at the thought. Nate's an amazing father, and I've never seen a man so excited about his unborn children.

"I need to—" I stop, eyes wide as I try to figure out what's happening. "Liz?"

"What, sweetie?"

"Either I'm peeing myself and I can't stop or my water just broke." A steady trickle of warmth runs down my leg.

She squeals and then claps. "Hospital. Come on. Let's go."

"We have plenty of time," I assure her. "Let's go across the street and get Nate."

"Are you sure? Should you be walking? Shouldn't I call your doctor?" She grabs her phone from her pocket. "I'll call Nate and then the doctor and then—"

"Liz." I put my hand on her arm. "It's going to be okay."

Biting her bottom lip, she wraps her arms around my enormous stomach and sighs. "I get to meet you two soon! You'll know me right away. I'm the cool one."

We grab my overnight bag and diaper bag and are halfway to the door when Nate and Asher walk in. Nate takes one look at me and the bag slung over Lizzy's shoulder and says, "Yeah?"

I nod, and before I can say anything, he pulls me into his arms, slides his hands into my hair, and kisses me.

"Knock it off!" Liz says. "You can suck face later. Now it's time to have some babies!"

EPILOGUE

NATE

Three Weeks Later

"Hey, Crane!" Asher calls, waving me over. "Is it done?"

I find a seat in the chair next to his and hand him the finished version of the song we've been hammering away at since August. Hanna's song.

"What about that?" I ask, pointing to a new line in the chorus.

"Yeah." He nods as he studies it. Then he grins. "Yeah, that could work."

I've written a lot of songs in my life and co-written even more, but none of them fought me as much as this one. Or maybe I'm the one who fought it. I wanted it to be about how sometimes loving someone means letting them go, and it didn't work. Months later, it's turned into a piece about how love is worth all the pain and heartbreak that comes before and after.

I knew, if I touched you, it'd be more than a kiss.
I need you. I'll feed you. I'll be your dying bliss.

Staring at the chorus, I sense her. I lift my head, and Hanna's smiling at me, my daughter in her arms. Next to her, Liz cradles my other daughter, gazing into her little face like a woman lost in love.

My daughters, Sophia and Josephine, are three weeks old today, and the family is over to welcome them home and celebrate their healthy births. I'm exhausted and sleep deprived and generally the luckiest bastard in the world.

"Are you two going to sing for us or not?" Maggie asks.

Asher winks at her. "Sure. We've even got something new." He strums the first chords of the song, and Hanna's eyes go wide. She's heard me working on it and begged me to sing it for her, but I told her she had to wait until it was done. I guess it's showtime.

You met me in the darkness and invited me to see
The path into the daylight wasn't what I thought it'd be.
I wanted to slay dragons for you but didn't understand
The dragons needing slaying were the ones inside my head.

I knew, if I touched you, it'd be more than a kiss.
I need you. I'll feed you. I'll be your dying bliss.
I'll be your superhero. I'd do it all for this.

The words aren't just perfect for the song. They're true. And when I look up from my guitar, I know she understands that every word is for her. She turns to Krystal and hands her the baby. Then she comes across the room and takes my hand.

"Are you ready to make good on your promise, angel?" I ask softly.

"What promise is that?"

I produce a ring from my pocket. It's an emerald-cut diamond framed by our daughters' birthstone. "Marry me. Be my wife and my family. Wear my ring."

She grins, and happy tears spill down her cheeks. "I was starting to wonder when you'd ask me."

THE END

ACKNOWLEDGEMENTS

First I have to thank my husband, Brian, and our kids, Jack and Mary. You make me remember what matters.

A huge thank-you to my friends and family for being amazing cheerleaders. From my siblings to my grad school buddies, to my ninety-six-year-old neighbor who has her visiting nurse hooked now, I couldn't ask for better book pimps.

To everyone who provided me feedback on this crazy twisty-turny plot—especially Heather Carver, Rhonda Helms, Adrienne Hogan, and Samantha Leighton. A special shout-out to Annie Swanberg, who threatened to write Here and Now fan fiction if I didn't have the guts to end this book the way it needed to end. You were right, of course.

Thank you to the team that helped me package this book and promote it. Sarah Hansen at Okay Creations designed my beautiful cover, and if I have my way she will do many, many more for me. To my editing team, Rhonda Helms, Mickey Reed, and Arran McNicol, you make my books better. To Chris, my assistant, who keeps me organized against all odds. Thank you to Christine at iHeartBigBooks for designing my gorgeous promo materials, and a massive shout-out to Julie with AToMR for organizing my promotional events. To all of the bloggers and reviewers who help spread the word about my books—you're amazing. Every one of you.

To my agent Dan Mandel and my foreign rights agent Stefanie Diaz for getting my books into the hands of readers all over the world—you're making my dreams come true.

To all my writer friends on Twitter, Facebook, and my various writer loops, thank you for your support and inspiration. Special thanks to the NWB—Sawyer Bennett, Lauren Blakely, Violet Duke, Jessie Evans, Melody Grace, Monica Murphy, and Kendall Ryan—you ladies make me smile on a daily basis!

And last but certainly not least, thank you to my fans all over the world. To those who read *Unbreak Me* and *Wish I May* and wrote begging for another New Hope story. To those who read *Lost in Me* and *Fall to You* and begged for early copies of *All for This*. You're the best fans an author could ask for. I couldn't do this without you and wouldn't want to. Thank you for buying my books and telling your friends about them. Thank you for being gracious and kind in your letters. And thank you for being the reason I have to pinch myself. You're the best, and you're the reason I get to live this dream.

~Lexi

All for This Playlist

Justin Timberlake—*Drink You Away*
Rihanna—*Stay*
Muse—*Madness*
Ingrid Michaelson feat. A Great Big World—*Over You*
A Great Big World—*Already Home*
Sam Smith—*Stay with Me*
Pink, Nate Reuss—*Just Give Me a Reason*
Ani DiFranco—*Falling Is Like This*
Norah Jones—*Come Away With Me*
Train—*Marry Me*
Oh Honey—*Be Okay*

What Lexi's Reading

I love reading almost as I love writing. Here are a couple books I'm looking forward to: *Sugar on the Edge* by Sawyer Bennett and *The Request Trilogy* by Marquita Valentine. Find the blurbs and a brief excerpt of each below.

Sugar on the Edge by Sawyer Bennett
About the Book:

He's utterly alone…

Tortured and existing in a dark spiral of despair, bestselling British author, Gavin Cooke, has come to the Outer Banks of North Carolina to escape the seedy lifestyle he had been living in London and in a desperate attempt to regain his writing focus. He's twisted, bitter and angry at the world. He's a loner… needing not a single thing other than his Scotch and a laptop upon which he can bang out his next erotic, dark thriller.

She's running in place and getting nowhere…

Savannah Shepherd's life is falling apart. Her dream of being a wildlife photographer seems a distant memory and she's barely able to make ends meet. Driving herself forward with no clear goals apparent, she's about ready to pack up her bags and head home with her tail between her legs.

Two unlikely lovers…

He's raw, forceful and a dirty talker. She's a flowers and romance type of girl. Yet within each other, they find a mutual craving that can only be satisfied by giving in to their desires for one another.

Lust turns into something more… something they were not looking for but tentatively accept. Will it be enough to push them past the obstacles of Gavin's bitter past?

Excerpt:

Savannah lets out a soft sigh from the couch, and I watch her intently. The hand across her stomach moves up, and she stretches both of them over her head, arching her back off the couch in a sleepy stretch. It pulls her T-shirt up higher, exposing more of her stomach and thrusting her breasts out.

The two glasses of scotch I've had haven't mellowed me enough that my dick doesn't take notice of the unintentional, but sexy move. It thumps against the zipper of my jeans with interest.

I wonder if I could seduce her… right now? I wonder if I gave into this attraction… this lust that's brewing for her, could the pounding of my cock between her legs drive her right out of my thoughts for good? Maybe that's what I need… just to fuck her, with raw, primal energy… enough to scare her away for good. Maybe then, I could quit thinking about her. She'd run away crying, her dignity shredded, and I could hire a new cleaning service and be done with her.

Savannah takes a deep breath, lets it out, and then goes still. I can't see if her eyes are open in the shadows where she lies, but by the measured movement of her chest, I think she's gone back down under.

Setting my empty tumbler on the table beside me, I stand up and walk over to the couch. I stare down at her, her face so serene and peaceful. I wonder if she's dreaming.

Without a second thought, I sit down on the edge of the couch, in a small area available to me by her left hip. Taking my finger, I stroke it over the skin of her stomach and say, "Sweet… it's time to wake up?"

She gives a soft moan in her sleep and arches her back off the cushions again.

And fuck, that's sexy.

And yeah, I definitely want to fuck her.

"Savannah," I call out to her softly and bring my hand up to her face, grazing my fingers over her temple. "You need to wake up."

Her eyes flutter open, immediately making contact with mine, and I let my hand drop away.

"She's alive," I murmur as she stares at me with dark eyes.

"What time is it?" she rasps out, turning her head to the left to look out the back glass door.

"Just after nine PM," I tell her. "You slept like a rock. I could have had my way with you, and you would have never known."

"Oh, yeah?" she asks skeptically, and with sleep still heavy in her voice. "Like what?"

Oh, little girl, the things I could have done to you.

I go for the shock factor to see what she does. Reaching my left arm behind me, I place my fingers on her calf. Her skin is warm and silky, and her breath hitches at the slight touch. "I could have skimmed my fingers up your leg, right past your knee... up your thigh," I tell her, moving my fingers up that same path I'm describing. When I get to the edge of her shorts, I halt my progress. "I could have inched my way right under these short little shorts... found the edge of your damp panties just to prove that you were having a sexy little dream while you were sleeping."

A tiny moan comes out of her mouth, and her eyes glitter back at me from the ambient light of the lamp reflecting in them. "You didn't do that," she says without any type of conviction at all... and is that a bit of longing I hear?

I finger the edge of her shorts. "I've done all kinds of dark and dirty things that your limited imagination could never fully appreciate. It would have been nothing for me to do that to you."

"Maybe so," she breathes out in a rush, "but you wouldn't have done that without my consent."

"Hmmm," I say thoughtfully, releasing the denim material and placing my fingers on her hot skin, feeling her muscles jump underneath my touch. "I'm wondering... would you give me your consent right now? Would you let me tunnel my fingers inside just a bit, let me see if your panties are damp because what I'm saying to you now is turning you on?"

The Request Trilogy by Marquita Valentine, *Book One*
About the Book
*** Roman Smith ~ Shopkeeper by day. Assassin by night. ***

The undercover Russian contract killer has never turned down an assignment that rids the world of scum… until his latest job targets an innocent man.

Refusing is not an option.

Everly Andrews, the sexy southern belle who saved him from dying and is completely unaware of his double life, has been marked as next on the kill list should he fail. There's nothing Roman won't do to keep Everly safe, even if it means losing her in the process.

Excerpt:

Everly rewards me with a tremulous smile. I allow my thumb to pass over a knuckle, and her breath hitches. She leans forward slightly, mahogany waves falling. Our eyes meet, and I'm helpless in this moment. The last time she was this close to me, I'd been shot.

Now, I'm perfectly healthy and perfectly willing to take her to my bed. Because of her, I haven't been with anyone in months. *Months.* The thought of using another as a replacement for her leaves my mouth as dry as ashes in a dead hearth.

"Your friend," she says, her lips inches from mine. Plump and pink.

Lickable. I want to devour her, starting at that mouth.

"He's browsing."

She covers my hand with hers, but not to pull it away. Instead, she squeezes, and my dick gets hard. I close my eyes. This is no way to react to her fear, but my body knows who's touching it.

"Have lunch with me on Friday."

My eyes pop open. "Pardon?"

"Lunch. You and me, we'll eat and talk about books and non-shooting things. We won't mention bullets or hospitals or nightmares of seeing a friend covered in blood," she says, her smile quivering at the corners.

"You had nightmares?"

She nods. "I didn't think I could ever come back here again."

"Why did you?"

A little shrug and she looks away. I turn her face back to mine with my free hand. Heat arcs between us, my thumb dusts her lower lip, and her mouth parts. I dip my finger in slightly, and her tongue touches the tip before she pulls away.

A groan escapes before I can stop it. My sweet *solnyshko.* "Love, tell me why you came back."

Other Titles
by LEXI RYAN

New Hope Trilogy
Unbreak Me
Stolen Wishes
Wish I May

The Here and Now Series (A New Hope Series)
Lost in Me
Fall to You
All for This

Hot Contemporary Romance
Text Appeal
Accidental Sex Goddess

Stiletto Girls Novels
Stilettos, Inc.
Flirting with Fate

Decadence Creek
Just One Night
Just the Way You Are

Coming Soon...

Something Reckless Series (A New Hope Series)
Something Reckless (Coming December 2014)
Something Real (Coming 2015)

Contact
LEXI RYAN

I love hearing from readers, so find me on my Facebook page at facebook.com/lexiryanauthor, follow me on Twitter @ writerlexiryan, shoot me an email at writerlexiryan@gmail.com, or find me on my website: www.lexiryan.com

CPSIA information can be obtained at www.ICGtesting.com
Printed in the USA
LVOW12s1614021014

406990LV00008B/1167/P